Apr 17

KINGDOM OF THE YOUNG

Fiction with a Nonfiction Coda

EDIE MEIDAV

SARABANDE BOOKS
Louisville, KY | Brooklyn, NY

The true Lesson of the Master, then, is, simply, never to venerate what is complete, burnished, whole . . . never to worship ripe Art or the ripened artist; but instead to seek to be young while young, primitive while primitive, ungainly when ungainly—to look for crudeness and rudeness, to husband one's own stupidity or ungenius.

—Cynthia Ozick

Library of Congress Cataloging-in-Publication Data

Names: Meidav, Edie, author.
Title: Kingdom of the young / Edie Meidav.
Description: First edition. | Louisville, KY : Sarabande Books, [2017]
Identifiers: LCCN 2016039500 | ISBN 9781941411414 (softcover : acid-free
paper)
Subjects: | BISAC: LITERARY COLLECTIONS / American / General. | FICTION /
Short Stories (single author). | FICTION / Literary.
Classification: LCC PS3563.E3447 A6 2017 | DDC 813/.54--dc23
LC record available at https://lccn.loc.gov/2016039500

Cover design and interior by Kristen Radtke.

Manufactured in Canada.
This book is printed on acid-free paper.

Sarabande Books is a nonprofit literary organization.

  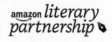

This project is supported in part by an award from the National Endowment for the Arts. The
Kentucky Arts Council, the state arts agency, supports Sarabande Books with state tax dollars and
federal funding from the National Endowment for the Arts.

BELIEVERS

KNAVES

DREAMERS

CODA

BELIEVERS

KINGDOM OF THE YOUNG
(10:15–10:35)

He is marching but losing the point, the rest of us falling behind the leader who can't help the slightly affected pointing lift of his left foot as he marches. Our commander, but we can't help noticing that about a half mile ago he dropped his pince-nez and none of us want to go pick it up and, true, at one point we swore allegiance to him, his bounty our bounty, his bread our bread, his trouble with the knee ours, but the problem has become that he is losing the point of the mission, having begun to hallucinate at night which means we see him through the pigskin tent, that strange gas-lamp silhouette of him hunchbacked and walking about with one strange pointing foot, and when he sleeps, he turns and cries the worst sort of epithets, things which, were you to hear them on a conventional battlefield, might chill your spleen to such an extent that you'd want to turn tail. Except turning tail is one thing we never do, he is our commander and not only have we sworn lifelong fealty to him, we promised we would make his time our time, his fantasies of bringing the enemy to their rotting knees our own, he is what we'd dreamt when still prone to childish pursuits such as fly-wing-burning and other wholesome occupations. Our commander, true, but inside him opens a great abyss which questions whether this whole mission is doomed, whether we will cross the mountain range and desert pass before finding the oasis, from there stumbling upon the absconded king's hideout at which the king, that dread king, will be beheaded with one fell swoop of our commander's knife, and, at this juncture, this is what I want to know, will there be an understanding among our whispering horde of how we should continue? *It is hard to know how to play the thing right,* our commander says when most confessional, pulling his beard late at night, *whether one is to push or pull, slide or slip, run or renegotiate.* And only a few of his trusted advisers, I among them, are allowed to hear these ostensible innards of his mind which runs on tracks so anointed that when he was six, I still just a wing-burner, our commander was already called a world leader and by the time he was twelve, he led a small troop, outdoing his father who only came to his own ruling post at seventeen. Now our commander is thirty, which seems to us quite old, and we believe he is fading somewhat in his impulses, questioning not only the motives of the entire project, but also, and far worse, starting to turn a suspicious eye upon each of us. It is not as if he lacks for good men in his troops: we number in the hundreds and have mastered archery, musketry, the art of hanging our laundry in orderly lines so that no one gets confused and takes another's codpiece. We are disciplined, polished to a high degree of spiff, the kind to understand what it means to look down someone's barrel and undertake war without falling into being the bleeding hearts who so often think first of their enemy's constitutions, wives and neighbors, pumping hearts and viscera, such thoughts and considerations those of lily-livered warriors who find it hard to withdraw sword from scabbard, intention from dormancy, action sloth. The problem with our troops is not our lily livers, no, rather that we have begun to pick up the malaise of our master, and we believe this has to do with our commander turning thirty, an age which makes us just as wary of him as he is becoming of us. We believe that when we come to the abandoned oasis and idyll of the dread desert king, we may actually kidnap the king ourselves (the king who, after all, is twenty-seven, deserving therefore to live at least a few more years), and will swoop that king, however aged, into our midst, buoy him aloft, carry him back to our kingdom where we will set up once again a kingdom solely of the young and for the young, a kingdom ruled by the young, and in our kingdom children shall frolic and beautiful narcissus flowers shall grow, and when the stems turn milky white and show signs of dying, we will dispatch our gardeners, men and women sensitive to signs of senescence, so that they may lop off whatever it is which might remind us that we too are not immune to the yearly march. We will paint our maidens fresh and rosy and when they too reach the wrong age, we will politely show them the exit. When bread grows stale, as men and women begin to stumble when reaching for a certain fact—what they had for breakfast yesterday morning, where they left their keys, how to make apple brown betty, how long it might take to travel to the neighboring kingdom if one were to harness two midsized and healthy moose for the journey—we will do what we can to bring them in line and also, always with the highest standard of courtesy, remind them with our gentle nod about all the joys farewell contains. And from the doorway will extend a chute, lined with greased velvet to make the passage all the more pleasurable. When those who have reached the age at which they besmirch our kingdom's ethos must leave, they will find the chute to be a not unpleasant midway, a furry but lubricated liminal zone in which one might reflect on errors. And once our former neighbors have slid down to the very bottom, there they will find further chance to reflect, in the form of a large reflecting pool, and along the perimeter of that reflecting pool filled with floating grayed narcissus flowers, with discarded bread crusts and lost watches, all those who have left our kingdom—we will not call them rejects, we never call anyone a reject—all of them will be free to sit and pull at their paling beards, scratch balding pates and keep their thin old-person ankles warm. Reflecting, our former neighbors, whom we would never in a million years call rejects, will marvel at all they got to see in the brief sweet span of their youth, free to rejoice at all they still recall, watching calendar pages fly off into their sputtering faces as in an old movie 1 2 3 4 5, mostly free to contemplate what exactly their sins were, all amounting to a particular sum: what they have done to abuse time. You see, even as I've told this story, using up precious minutes, the fact remains: we have no time for such sinners in our holy kingdom of the young.

ROMANCE; OR, BLIND IN GRANADA

She was a bohemian girl with lots of life to live fast. Only in her early twenties but making up for time lost to who knows what. To books or the slow Cheshire-cat vanishing act effected by her best friend, to a dreamy childhood with the wrong doors unlocked like her outsize painting ambition or the inability to trust those she knew, apart from her great-uncle of the round head and romantic aspiration who died but first told her in his French accent that he wanted to leave her a little money saved up from teaching so that when she found herself alone in a funeral-home room with his ethylated body, he appeared to wink and say go ahead now, enjoy yourself the way I always meant to. Her uncle who read books in many languages and taught English to foreign girl students from Asia while never foregoing his strong Sex Appeal cologne because how could he keep himself from falling in love with students to the point that the cashier at the local cinema knew him by the line he used whenever he took a new one out: But are there bigger discounts for sexy senior citizens? He had gotten poorly embroiled with the last Korean student who would not so much as kiss him if he did not marry her, saying: The cow won't give milk unless you feed it, this student his greatest disappointment since only death separated him from the love he thought might one day still be his, a love first whispered by French poetry and later mouthed by smoke rings in American kisser films he'd managed to see back when the Congo was still the Belgian. He had once dreamed of becoming a painter in Tahiti and so there remained a whole heap of unused pleasure in him which he ended up bequeathing the girl. With this sum she planned to go to Europe because she too had read a book about an enchantress in Spain and a book about traveling boys and hijinks that made escaping the slate-gray a correct course of action. While everyone had told her stories about the Alhambra in Granada, saying so determinedly it really was the place she had to go, a near peak of European civilization, the last place in which so many ideologies about love and faith interpenetrated, such possibility flourishing in that moment if you could only travel back and alter later history in which all streams continued in their straitened way. But you must go to Granada, they chimed, while she kept opening her Spain guidebook to the quotation from the medieval king who said there is no pain worse than being blind in Granada and so it was confirmed, the message, especially as both parents had started to dwindle at their edges, death moving in toward the core: clearly there was no pain worse than living life too slowly.

Once there, she bought a small guitar from a courtly guitar-maker who asked if she would like to come by some night despite his wife and colicky grandson while also not knowing where someone might take guitar lessons authentic to Andalucía. Leaving the guitar-maker's small cramped studio, carrying the guitar, she nonetheless felt as if she were in a story she had read as a child about a happy pig named Pearl who carried in her satchel a magic bone, and the girl meant to speed life a little by getting coffee on her way back to a hostel populated by Viking descendants when instead a gypsy intercepted her with his El Greco face, all massive drooping eyes and aquiline nose as he unhanded her of the new guitar and started singing to her right there to her in the Plaza

Mayor where she knew she had landed in the very center of the thing she had envisioned but had not named.

You have killed me with your walk, he sang, strumming her guitar, stretching it out—camino—o—o-o, chin wobbling at each O. Behind each tremble, a gaggle of ancestors lined up with the question of whether he could live up to them. He did his best. After his song was done he asked with some seriousness if she might come live with him in the small caves up above where tourists walk, white dwelling caves honeycombed into the hills facing the Alhambra which perhaps a king had made as a testament of love to his wife, a story that endured in a way that made her question if she would ever really know what it meant to fall in love despite her schooling in all the songs, because what had she ever known? Granada was either stripping her bare or layering on a new scrim since she was feeling more or at least someone else's more. While the gypsy sang premature songs of love her way, she had almost been able to see him or had been looking at him through blinds, unsure since both possibilities melted as he sang, and of course it was both risky and imaginary to throw yourself into another's thrall when anyway wasn't it always chemical? She had been curious about people throwing their hats down before her but didn't know if she had ever thrown down anything or just responded. Was she to be so deprived of experience? Love, to love, to fall in love. She had climbed mountains but never fallen. Others had been obsessed, sometimes with her, and was she only to know escape and absconding? Yet what was the strange thrill of the gypsy singing to her? It had to do with all stories conjoining in a spot just above her navel as if she were not on the road seeking but at both source and end, dead center inside a kaleidoscope. This itself is a story about the problem with the picturesque and how it links with the picaresque, and how certain girls are prone to confusing the two, going out to wander the landscape with something like one of Claude Lorrain's mirrors turned backward at the landscape. If something seems correct enough in its set details they forgive enough to think: here might lie fulfillment, the idea working until fulfillment itself gives them the lie.

At night the gypsy and she did the deed, only one of them blushing in the dark on the floor in the gypsy cave though somewhere she was also numb because she didn't stop to ask what, for all his singing about her eyes and voice, her smile and a chance at amor, amor, what about him was fulfillment? She had chosen this, it was no rape, he was dead center with her but was there any vastness other than mammal embrace or the satisfaction of being in a cave with an avatar of Granada reaming her out of thinking? There was something they both tried to extract on the unseen side of the other, a mystery she would never solve ever, his animal breath in her ear, her face on the stone floor, the two of them more ancient because of the Alhambra beyond the window, the girl imagining him her conqueror while at the same time being the filmgoer curious about what the next scene in the movie would bring. She almost knew enough to name it and woke the next morning inquisitive, her cheery guitar next to her in its opened blue plush case, one she loved as it also seemed to promise an interesting future. The gypsy took her to a special tetería where they sat on beaded pillows and he drank Moroccan tea broken only by song when he needed to illustrate a point about love, attachment, loss. What did they talk about? Guitars, his family, I love you so, singing in full display, throat full, eyes flashing. Midday they went to see his stern aunt rehearsing and there encountered the source of the wobble, the quirk coming from another singer, his romantic uncle. To sing gypsy guitar, you had to hurt and when you hurt most you were to open your mouth wide and let out the longing she had read about, duende another flame over centuries. How good to hurt and know loss, to feel passion-ion-ion, tremble, vibrato, melisma, words that appeared in the girl's head like keepsakes from another realm. There she was deep in the cave with the gypsy family, a dusty moment out of time only she got to applaud since no one had any idea where she was, while no one in the gypsy caves seemed surprised to see her, the acceptance traveling far enough to create belonging. She had come along, toting her guitar as both a coin of the realm and earnest passport, something they had never seen held by a tourist. The

aunt happened to be a beautiful narrow stern bird skilled in fortunetelling who grasped the girl's rib cage and waist to calibrate the instru-
ment, telling the girl she could be useful not at babies but at dancing.
Meaning the girl lagged only a few centuries behind. Was this then
the story the girl was in, in which she would learn to be a flamen-
quería from this stern woman who brooked no fools? Good at dancing, bad at babies, fallen in love? Late afternoon the gypsy brought
her to the small blue-painted subterranean room, blue to keep away
the evil eye, in which his mother perhaps lived with his older sister
and a bunch of children with parentage impossible to align, in order
for the gypsy's mother to explain to the girl all the grimy details of
one granddaughter's illness with such compelling force that her eyes
barred any new story, despite the chaos around her capable of fixing
on one tale with its point shriveling away, one the girl felt she almost
reached but did not. No es comprensible, she wanted to say, instead
saying, yes, claro, I understand. Afterward, along the road back to
the gypsy's little cave, he beckoned her to stop at a small counter of a
restaurant where they shared a cheese sandwich as if already a couple
with life behind and ahead in which he would wear his wifebeater
t-shirt, his skin glossy under her fingertips, and later with her useful
waist she would dance for his aunt but really for him, and on her
epitaph you could read about acceptance, belonging, having traveled
far from your original ideas. When it came time to pay for the meal,
she told the counterboy, another cousin of the gypsy, that it was her
gift. As if on cue the gypsy unrolled a song about how he could never
thank her for the brightness of her eyes, a song perhaps made up on
the spot despite the legacy of the chin wobble. In the full of afternoon
they went back to his cave in theory to put her guitar down but more
to lie once more on the floor of the cave and spill acrid red wine from
a leather bota into their mouths before entangling, rectangles of sun
stretched long over skin, his chest almost a smooth boy's though light
caught the end of each hair, her foreigner's hand rippling over the
brilliance. You will learn guitar well, he said, laughing. Did a bubble of a question start in her throat then? When they were done,

she emerged into an unusual hour, everything lit from within, little
fairy lights popping on, strung up outside the white plastered cave
doors facing the Alhambra, the palace tucked into its hillside just as
they were tucked into theirs. Everyone along the gypsies' winding
cobblestoned road up the mountain knew flamenco was good business. Produce romance for people and they get happy, said her gypsy,
they pay more. Every little cave they passed had candlelit tables for
two. Candles are important! he started to sing, hand on the back of
her neck where only an hour earlier he had been holding her down.
Now she knew he was making everything up in the received mode,
his family singing him as it had sung for generations while she felt so
moorless. As the sun sank behind the Alhambra, the tourists started
to rise in an obedient swell, twos, fours, family units up into the ark
of romance, craning their necks, and through their eyes she saw the
charm of the day lit up, the glowing white of the caves and she in it
with them, able to see both tourists and gypsies, the double frame
giving her courage less about some story and more about this life
of hers not skulking to the fringe of things. All this had happened in
little more than a day. Her insides sore but in a good way, a tiredness
under her eyes carrying everyone else's reportage though she no longer had to tote around the contours of herself. The gift the gypsy had
given her was dissolving a bit and she wished to help the cause of dis-
solution by welcoming the craning tourists into the aunt's cave while
standing aside so as not to take a seat from paying customers while
the stern bird began her dance, heels tatting a pulse as the tragic face
twisted to tell of horror, loss and union so doomed you too could live
at the molten core. The gypsy played with his uncle and because this
time the uncle gave his all the gypsy did too, fusing in music so that
the tourists shivered in the cave because they too lived at the heart
of experience, Spain, the Roma. After, she helped fold seats and then
went back to a different uncle of the gypsy's and until late, for free,
for no other outsider but her, bands of gypsies drank and sang, making ribald, inclusive comments that named her almost an honorary
man due to foreigner status, one of few women in that room, so many

rough hands placed over hers to teach her guitar, because she was the ilk of girl who was going to learn flamenco guitar. The next morning by some arrangement she did not quite understand they went to some other uncle's cave, bigger and better whitewashed, where the uncle told her he was the last of a rare line of seers while her gypsy stood by. The uncle explained that he needed to look right below her breasts to determine her fortune and because she was very much midexperience she lay on the table, shirt off, letting the uncle tell her fortune from small invisible marks he could ascertain only if he got close enough to either kiss or scrutinize her skin, all while her gypsy stood looking out the door with his face telegraphing an important errand he had almost forgotten and in this the question in her throat grew, she wanted to ask something but had no clue how to form it.

Once the fortunetelling session was over, they stopped by his mother's who reminded her of the sick granddaughter and how the illness had worsened after which her gypsy suggested they go get coffee in the square where she ran into a friend from school named Lincoln and his new French girlfriend Nathalie. Because they invited her with them to the beach somewhere for a day or two, she made apologies to her gypsy because she needed to think and gathered her backpack from the hostel's locker since despite his singing entreaties she had not fully decided to go on living with him. And so she went with Lincoln and Nathalie to stay in their tent on a beach and at night shifted her attention from the massive caterpillar heave of their sleeping bag or how unequal the two of them were, Lincoln less besotted with Nathalie while surely that French girl deserved better. Why had they asked her along after all? The triangle confused since by day she loved Nathalie's broad-cheeked wistful charm, so bruised and Gallic, all of them rumpled and the two girls buying eternal friendship bracelets from someone on the beach but after a couple of days of sandy headstands, fish dinners and talks containing the magic of the future in which they would never again meet, she said goodbye and headed back, feeling herself wise and weary on the train to Granada. In the main café in town she ran into her gypsy, handsome and magically wearing a green bright button-down shirt she thought she had lost in her hostel. Maybe she had left it at the cave? All he kept saying with a kind of force was: Did you not bring me anything from your trip? How could you not bring me anything? Gone were the songs and wobble. In that second she may have understood him saying that her main failure was that she had not yet given his mother money for the sick grandkid and that for him she may have been something just a bit more or less than a walking dollar sign. Whatever he had professed before, during or after lay intimately close to a performance of feeling. I cannot let you go-o-o. She had windmilled into his story in which feeling was king. Would it matter that she had been set in his midst? After her, would there not be other travelers, toting their guitars, waists, hunger? After he left, she stayed in the café, mournful. A drummer she had seen in a circle, a drummer from Sierra Leone named Prince, came up to ask why so sad? And she told him and watched his moonlit drum circle that night before going to stay on his floor where she pretended to sleep when he began to touch her bent elbow after which she became the one living with him, eating peanut sauce with rice next to the hands of all his friends also dipping into one bowl. The drummer played bass guitar, a simple unskilled stuttered reggae one-two, but really loved drumming more and said he wanted to marry her which seemed a plausible version until the day she took him to the doctor for his cough and there in the waiting room he told her that he always thought the children of a blonde woman and a black man were the most beautiful so that she saw he lived in a saga that had little to do with her and so returned to Connecticut where at the post office she kept getting letters saying I want to come, I really want to marry you, but did not keep up correspondence because too easily she recognized the particular American fairytale the drummer wanted to live. And when years later her children called to her from downstairs, in another story she probably failed to recognize, a heated moment of dissatisfaction, she came across these yearning letters nestled into the blue plush case with the guitar long since broken, the blue still so untouched and bright, something you might pet to make the fur angle to catch the light, while she considered what yarn she might be able to spin for these children about the great and almighty Alhambra or the song of the gypsies but then realized, too, she had never once seen the Alhambra from the inside and anyway would whatever tale she might summon ever count as anyone's idea of a gift?

THE KING OF BUBBLES

Overheating in the tub next to the pool, birthday next day, a face notches less recognizable each morning. Meeting someone these days means whoever you say you once were matters less. Once you get older it becomes easier to say who you are not, a long scroll to be written there, longer than your life actually lived. So many paths turned away from: never a king of industry, for one, that path abandoned before anyone finished saying Constantinople, but who even said Constantinople anymore anyway? Once you may have been a history major, breathing the dust of old editions while full-tilt windmilling at the future. Now you have become a service-minded figure near retirement going around enlightening the masses. So some efforts fizzled, could have happened to anyone. These days, you wave your card, a flag of defeat. Educational consultant, you being an older male consulting re: what again? These days, you flash your hanging badge like you too could qualify for an IEP write-up, almost like cute smiley or slack-jawed special-ed kids with their notes from home dangling on their chests. Please be sure Muffy wears mittens when the thermometer drops below twenty because she has Raynaud's syndrome.

Or: Don't let Ricardo stare too long at screens because of his Irlen syndrome. While your syndrome might be despair or call it a blood-sugar lull circa eleven most mornings and later again at four and most Sunday afternoons once tasks are done. Real task, of course, is to stitch together a life above despair, like those stakes in a hammock you tried putting up each summer for your sons, a device damned from the get-go. Once the hammock snapped on their mitts and you were blamed, why not, you were capable of absorbing all, you the half-brawny man polite and absorbent, standing ready. As a kid, the best report cards called you polite, but what good do manners do anymore? You pushed your politeness into consultancy to warm your wallet while you consulted about what again? Too much of your professional advice begins with the phrase *what I have seen is that.* A gentle drumroll of wisdom wrested from syncopated years. One of your sons, the angry eldest, took the hammock off your hands, shepherding it to the dump while the other sons send seasonal gifts: a massaging armchair, a car-seat back support, a panic button, gifts meant to shore up and not shred old dad, but do they think you're some lonely stiff to be pitied? All three sons busy swaggering toward the unfinished freeway of their future while you sit on a throne of beads with a design ripped off from a porn store, a gift from the least estranged, the savvy middle son who never brags of a great childhood, none of them do, but why care when yours also lacked note, singular trauma or exaltation, obvious war scars? Anomie and distance also pock a person! And if you have ended up at a career pinnacle, teaching people how to serve the children of the future, the truth is you probably surrendered long ago, the first time you saw tests fail the brightly underserved. Probably or never, all the above, none.

Sink a little lower in the hot tub. This new year includes a massive self-improvement kick because why not link with the lemmings? Resolve to resolve by joining this mildewed dank warren of a health club where your point on the spectrum of age clarifies itself within the family of man, flapping paps in the locker room, all the hearty male enfolding of good cheer, no towel slaps, only old men folding towels to place under veinous feet. Never before have you seen men place towels under their feet anywhere but within these labyrinthine halls, so might it be true these men know something about staph and habits of self-preservation which fail you? As the gym had grown, it had accommodated, just like you and the towel-footed, this gym with vascular corridors that keep dropping another room at the end of another artery. Traversing the place is to navigate a maze of aspiration, wafting limey cologne and acid sweat, one of the scents more regretful, but which?

Much better to be in this swampy gym tub than in the huge, hygienic and better-equipped place in town filled with fledglings, in which, on each of the few times you entered, you were marked not within the family of man but rather with perma-age, all the rings on a petrified tree. Many of those gym's kids may have been students for whom you once sacrificed, but what again had been your altar, what had you risked, what had been the terms of sacrifice and had you ever really agreed at the outset? Or what did it mean anyway, to make someone's education better? Who needed life lessons more, slumpers in the classrooms or you, and do you anyway believe in measuring anyone's schooling? Does it matter who sits in which configuration or whether students are taught toward the test, mainstreamed or segregated? What anyway does not come down to a fight against isolation?

The grown children align with their mother. That is their truth, as one said, and they hold that waterproof truth tight against everything and you, especially since last year when papers finally went through, papers that could have gone through twenty years ago at your first dalliance. Here you are lacking both a note from home or much of any home at all, taking as evidence the recently rented railroad apartment, fairly unfurnished, in which you sleep, not having reached the ramen and peanut-butter-with-a-spoon phase if having already skidded into the open-newspaper-and-older-trash stage, your own metric on no assessment scale yet devised.

Some guy named Karl, beyond everyone else's yardsticks, goes around town in an admirably huge tent-like camel jacket. How does he keep it all together? That jacket so unstained? Wearing pink watershoes, he looks at no one over his immaculately tended handlebar moustache while wielding before him paperbacks of unusual provenance, a field map to the stars or the Dordogne, once *The Magic Mountain*, the book always changing, its surprise consistent as the frequency with which you find the guy sideways, lying on a carpet in a local drugstore or bookstore, taking upon himself a cleaning task involving the dismantling of some aspect of the store. And why not? Managers let him be because Karl is a good guy, they say, and yours is a progressive town, allowing all comers and takers if mostly the latter. Perhaps you might be considered a taker and Karl is a free-for-all giver. A clerk will say: Oh yes, there goes Karl cleaning my missed spot! After which the clerk goes on to mourn what this town used to be back when people cared more for their neighbors.

Karl knows something. How is it that from the hot tub at four on a Wednesday you find yourself in full-on Karl envy? The guy has his place. Touchpoints. Maybe the thing is to find places to set down, good as a spaceship determining to teeter on one particular mountain rim. Just today, on the way to the gym, there Karl had been, striding purposeful down the street past the pizza place, holding in one hand a rotted grapefruit and in the other a book with a hot pink cover, both with such a firm grasp: to speak your job's jargon, his hands are permanently tasked.

Just then it comes over you to notice the girl across the tub, though usually you might not, except that is one fulsome lie, you still always notice girls, inappropriately, except or especially during a dalliance, your noticing with its own life, a rising and falling torqued empire noted in no history book. Could you be forgiven? To move toward life: When could someone have declared that wrong? What empires would have never risen had emperors quashed all life urge? While your gift as a consultant lay in how readily you noted what others could not. People on the job used to call you Bug, as in Bug who noticed everything, this their praise for your ability to analyze. To have eyes only for one? How could noticing many have become a crime?

But how confusingly this hot tub girl stares back. Not like you are deformed. On a spectrum, you are no Toulouse-Lautrec or whoever that runty painter with the stubby legs and hypertrophied manhood was, you being more the opposite, but there you have two hazel eyes unblinking at you. Gleaming beautiful eyes and perhaps the sneer the young use as a talisman to ward off the old and vampiric. She looks away because it must be too hard to take you in. Fine and well though *fuck her* rises as well, plums pushed forward in her plum bathing suit, so why bother staring when you are not such a terrible specimen and not just because you send year-end contributions for heifers or leave ramen and peanut butter in brown bags for the Scouts' hunger drive. Some have said you are not exactly an irritant. Easy on the eyes, your last dalliance commented, hair less black but so what, you aren't yet at the hair-dye or folded-towel-under-feet stage, so what could be so disconcerting to Miss Plum, probably in her midtwenties, few disappointments known, Miss Hazel Plum who must have had her share of swimming lessons, being daddy's favorite, probably a cheerleader, skin that smooth brown suggesting more nurture than nature, tanning salons, G-string perfection.

A small boil starting in the chest and not from the hot tub. Damn if you are not ready to get out if not ready for her to see too much, even if you are no Toulouse-Lautrec but the opposite, you with long legs, good at least one part of you stayed semivaliant against gravity, but foolish to give in when you have fought bigger fights and won.

Believing you know others' thoughts happens to be your occupational hazard. As a young man, before the wife and joyless lawyer paraded in with their papers, there had been that much older lover with her infirmities of the flesh you could not help seeing as a betrayal, a moral sloth and admission of chaos, a hazed attention to which you would never succumb. Freckled arms—not you! Though was it the case that this Plum with her stare might be mocking you as if slothful, today, on your birthday? Clearly she too could be, taken to pieces. This hot tub only big enough for one of us. Thought-telegraphing her way: One day, Plumette, the sun will set on your empire. You too will be old. Try looking elsewhere but this Plum but her eyes stay too bright. Behind in the big pool, ten dancing geriatric Esther Williams types in the big pool aim for arabesques, older women treating the pool as if it were a kiddie amusement park like the kind to which you used to take the sons, women being commanded by a young instructor marching poolside, exhorting them to wield odd foam swords. These Esther Williams people had gotten some memo you had not. Time to learn the moves, ladies. Swish swish wield, slide pump reach. A few smiling men among the Esthers. Declawed, denutted. Reach a particular birthday and suddenly everyone learns old-people pool moves? Not you. That tree of knowledge you could defy. Better to stay in blissful ignorance, though this gym has a way of seeming like old-people purgatory in which there is no way to avoid knowledge. Swish swish reach. Higher! The instructor shouting: Give me some life, people! What you know to do in a pool is crawl which is how it will stay. The crawl, if barely. Not even a flip at the end of a lap. Just touch the edge, turn, perform another lap with, okay, sometimes an affirmation in your head. What is so wrong with that? You listen to the audio in the car. *I am strong*, then crawl along, *Strong! Strong!* a highly peaceful repetition to consider while swimming. Afterward you feel yourself a better man. If someone tested your immune system, you would be found younger, the way they found that people at a reunion hear gossip and music from their youthful days and suddenly their immune system strengthens. So what do these types find in their old-people aqua-dance? Community? Their energetic instructor prancing poolside, maximus bared to indoor elements and older gazes, exhorting them: Greater height, friends! Shouting over a soundtrack with a repetitive chorus: Love shack, baby, love shack.

Across the far end of the pool, obeying the song's injunction, a tall boy nuzzles his ginger-haired companion, actually sliding under her hair so as to better kiss the back of her neck, both filled with that unblemished self-regarding performance of youth, deep in the morning-after prize that will continue for a few months until it fades, you want to tell them: Love shack, baby, sure, enjoy your little moment.

Probably these two are also students for whose education you
had sacrificed hours on a tired rear, hours spent sitting which turns
out steals minutes from your ischemic health. For you there will be
no prizes, just decency its own reward, though it remains unclear
under which banner decency parades. Plum with her short gamine
hair has actually gone so far as to turn the back of her neck to you,
and what film does the line come from, j'ai toujours aimais ta nuque,
and if you only took more omegas or vanquished the right computer
games, your memory would give you back the full-color romance of
seeing that film with the wife in your early years. Here you have Plum
turning her nuque like she really cannot stand one more moment
looking at you, the geezer, and so what if you too could nuzzle such
a neck, surely that nuque much nuzzled, by whom though, a young
pimply lothario or a big floppy sugar daddy, or maybe she was into
women like your wife says she maybe now is. Comment allez-vous?
What is Plum doing now? A subtle ballet move, another fool mistak-
ing the future as a ladder, one big set of rungs for latitudinal acts of
self-improvement.

The boil too much, your homeostasis a difficult act to maintain.
You may be losing the battle but will not surrender the war. You cannot get out of the tub and let Plum see you: a frog who cannot exit
water turned up by degrees. She is the one doing it to you, like your
ex-wife had also, chopping off her hair, what you had once loved,
at your last dalliance. Deprive you she would and had. In your current state, could you take young Plum seeing you? No and nuga-
tory, choice clearly Hobson's. No choice. Just stay. Boil off the skin.
Why not. Peeled old chicken. They will find you there, the opposite
of WWII gallant soldiers found almost completely preserved in the
ice melting off the Italian Alps. Poor consultant, scalded alive on his
birthday, cause held tight as the flagpole at Iwo Jima.

So finally her ballet finishes and she starts to get out. Let her. Let
her rise, when little does she know how decisive this moment is, let
her parade with that minimus. As if for once magical thinking actually grants you the triumph of match point. Getting out of the tub

with her perfection, she knows you watch. Would it be a good idea to say something to show who is in charge? *Can't stand the heat, get out of the fire.* Nix on the cliché. *Weather too much?* Probably better to stay silent, enjoy conquest, eyes manly, consummating the meal, love shack subsiding, an uncanny silence descending at your coup.

Tugging at her bathing suit, the girl already stands at the chairs, fiddling with a towel, this Plum in profile so you can savor the overthrow. Although of course a person could wonder on which side downfall had fallen? With a delicacy so careful it could wrench, almost beautiful, she shudders away. Away from you, from the rest of the pool, from everyone—doing what, after all? This is what she does: she removes first one and then another glass eye, granting only you the vision of her face. Two gouged slits no monster could envy. Some optician somewhere had crafted hazel. She is slow now, tinkering with a careful white case. Before you exhale, she yanks goggles over all you cannot fathom. After that, the swimming cap. And then · stands at the pool's edge, as ready for her laps as a knife.

THE BUDDHA OF THE VEDADO

For seven years in prison every day he had a chair to himself. He had a chair and a desk and even a private room in which he could kick his heels up on a desk. Yuzniel had a friend on the outside falsify a certificate saying that he had been a geography and history teacher so he got to teach classes four times a week, which was hard, being as he was a high school dropout, but he had no problem getting students to come to classes, people liked him, part of his problem being he could get anyone to believe, always made himself ready for anyone. That he got to move around and have some private space meant everything in prison, and when he wanted something, he was diligent, which might have counted for at least half of why I had fallen in love.

We met as scraggly kids in our neighborhood with its sidewalks torn up by roots, the one where you have state employees working eight hours a day with a machete trimming snatches of grass so that tourists at the fancy hotels facing the seawall boulevard don't feel they left too much home behind. Even if all the neckless men from Italy or Switzerland trip as they totter out of their hotels, their reward is they get to lean on their mulattas, never technically hired, and we knew what the exchange meant about the demon capitalism: curves on certain girls meant capital to come or capitalism spent.

It is not hard to fall in love in Cuba but it is equally easy to fall out, like that round-robin salsa only the best male dancers do where they twirl their girls with that bored face of the best salseros, the girls endlessly switching partners, the dance really about the expertise of the men though the girls' compliance masks greater skill. This may be why we have one of the world's highest divorce rates and may also have to do with the circulation necessary to any island's inner flow, the one that makes us depend on that influx of foreign neckless wonders, their loud vacation shirts tenting over their tummies as they eye their disco girls.

I did not meet my local boy at a disco but instead outside school where those without mothers shouting them home could ride a crumbly plaster wall where we sat stealing time by drinking and pretending to be adults. Yuzniel teased me like a brother whenever I wore eyeliner I had swiped from my older sister but I teased him for wearing the boys' beige uniform with hems so high because of his lankiness, our pestering meaning we kept full radar on each other afternoons anywhere, in classes, halls, fields. Even if we pretended we were just two people in our group, we knew what the other one thought so no one was shocked when, right before he dropped out, we hooked up.

His mother went crazy three years later and ended up in the hospital our leader said brought disgrace to Cuba because it turned out the director ignored workers swiping sheets, medicine, food. It took some busybody American agency snooping to find the crazies dying of starvation and cold middle of the half-century of our revolution that had never stopped. Yuzniel was less ashamed of his mother than our leader was about the hospital. No one held having some crazy genes against anyone in our country, especially not against my boy who behaved like the humble mayor of our zone, always helping even the lowest of the low, one more of the revolutionary slogans we loved to mock. Billboards around us advertised the thoughtful pensamientos of our leader or José Martí or any other of our national heroes and these were our favorite blackboards, the ones we loved to scrawl on, bizarre comments inserted into such holy words so the tang of teenage mischief filled our veins. But really there was no other country for us: we liked to say the people, never its rulers, made the place. You only had to look at all the neckless men who understood our charms, even if we knew our island had basically become some kind of beautifully outfitted jail. Most of the people we knew were in line for some Miami uncle or Boca aunt to send word even if the old-timers liked saying they were diehard fidelistas, humanitarians, comunistas, people pretending revolution stirred their moros y cristianos siempre. But of course people fool themselves staying in a bad situation, liking to tell themselves someone wiser knows what's best.

At first I felt sorry for Yuzniel. His mother gone pure crazy and we all knew his older sister had played jinetera, outfitting herself with jangly earrings and tight jeans before finding herself a rich Swiss at the hotel down our street, the one that years later, after the pope came to Havana to lecture our leader about our morality problem, took up policies barring girls like her from even entering the front door alone. Back in her time, things were still open so she got out and ended up in Switzerland, sometimes sending home remissions to her little brother who was being raised by their demented grandfather who used the love-money to have big parties, whooping it up and only occasionally loaning some to Yuzniel whenever his grandson wanted to give someone starter cash.

Naturally any boy like this might go wild. Yuzniel used to come to school back when he was fourteen with hair in braids tight to his skull, drinking watered-down aguardiente out of a little silver flask with the Che face on it wearing off from exposure to cheap rotgut. Back then Yuzniel was pure edge, not yet the saint he became. It was hard not to be drawn to him and because I was popular with the other girls, I got him and for this my rank went up even more.

Never give me advice, he told me from the start, that's one thing, Yanet, I got to listen to my own master, I can't have anyone above me.

So when he decided to quit school and imitate Juan Carlos, the guy in his tipped fisherman's cap, the one we'd seen living it up down the avenue, the one we whispered was selling drugs to foreigners, of course I couldn't keep myself from telling him he was heading down the wrong path.

Come on, Yanet, you're supposed to be different, he said. We were Generation Y and so everyone had Y names, though at first Yuzniel's mother had wanted to call him Lazaro because his birth had been so difficult. Difficult as opposed to what, I wonder? He was born like we all were, yanked out by forceps a few years before the Special Period which happened when the Soviets pulled their support and our whole island started lacking forceps, clothes, soap, or goods, only rice, beans, and all the sugar you could die for.

In a way, my Y did what was smart. He didn't want to go the way of teachers diving into dumpsters to find something usable or the doctors selling lemonade or sewing kids' shoes on the street. He saw Juan Carlos was up to something else and that something Yuzniel wanted. As I mentioned, he was never anything but enterprising. To stay in the system as it wanted him to stay, hope to be some clerk making at most twenty-five dollars a month and figuring out how to survive by odd jobs on the side, you would have to be dumb. So Yuzniel did what any thinking man would do. At night he started selling small bags to the same tourists in the hotels whose mulattas needed a little extra in order to get it on, just some pot and cocaine, and this despite the daily reflections of our leader in the party paper about the evils of other countries and how we in Cuba were pure and above drugs, this when about half the men you meet on any day before ten in the morning have that little sting of rum or aguardiente on their breath, this despite the way we're allowed to sip our coffee mindlessly all day to not fall down the pit I started to know the day Yuzniel was caught.

You have to admire our leader. He had caught wind of the drugs rampant on the island and organized an island-wide sting between four and five in the morning one January which got thousands of dealers thrown into jail. Yuzniel at first was caged up with just dealers but then because of overcrowding they moved him after six months into the prison for rapists and murderers. That first morning he hit on the plan of becoming a history and geography teacher. My only goal is to get out, he told me right after we got married, part of his plan to get us time together, three hours a month of conjugal visits. Of course I made sure not to get pregnant if I had to be alone on the outside. I was working as a shopgirl and I'd come to him wearing the patterned stockings that only nurses and shopgirls get to wear and he would be so happy to see me, his narrow face lit into being more like a big happy dog who wanted to jump all over me even before the guard left us alone to our privacy.

I brought him whatever he needed, even the false certificate and books to study, I waited, and when he was let out one year early for good behavior as a teacher, who took the bus with him to his brother's home? We lived there with his brother and wife and their new baby until the lack of privacy just got too hard and I insisted Y open up some packets of the drug money he had hidden away and find us a new apartment, a tricky feat when we are only allowed to trade to the same size apartment and in fact nothing belonged to Yuzniel anymore, even the house of his grandparents had been swallowed by the government given his sister's total disappearance from the family's cause. Of course at that time she was suffering, having tried to divorce her neckless Swiss man but the Swiss guy had gotten so angry he had stolen her passport, even her clothes and money, and so for a few years she had been forced to rely on the goodness of the few Cubans she had met in Geneva and despite the tough times was doing her best to get back to Havana.

While things were looking up for me and Yuzniel. With some financial lubrication, we managed to get ourselves a place not far from his brother and our old-time crumbly wall and because the leader had just lifted the restrictions on people having their own businesses, just a little, or rather the leader's brother pushed him into it, we all got a break and could open up a little snack shop, hiring some of Yuzniel's ex-cons to work it, right near the hotel where his sister had bagged

her man, just a place for people to get a little coffee and pan con torti-
lla or croqueta or whatever they liked. And we were getting the hang
of the business, bribing the health inspector and electricity inspector
and the whole thing was starting to take off.

I never take anything for granted, he would say in the morning,
kissing me. Every time I breathe fresh air, every time I take a sip of
water, I realize all I could not have. Then he'd correct himself: What
we could not have. Together. You waited, Yanet baby, and I will never
forget that, I owe you.

And I would feel lucky because though I'd spent seven years
waiting out what my mother who'd made her own bad choices still
scolded me for, calling them seven petals stolen from the flower of my
youth, he and I ended up together again and better, my boy swearing
he would never touch selling drugs. Now that he knew the bad side
of bad, I could breathe easy.

Which is of course the way things go, right, the point when you
relax starts things spilling over. Wherever he was, Yuzniel played
mayor, answering this one's debt, picking up the cell to fix another's
water issue, calmly meeting everyone's need, which let him survive
prison without anyone laying a finger on him, his ring of friends
keeping its members protected. Clearly, on the outside, I didn't offer
enough of a ring to protect him. In our building lived the daughter
of one of our high school friends and she invented some kind of mad
attraction for him, throwing herself at his feet when her own father
died. Like a crazy from his mother's asylum she wanted Yuzniel, a girl
not even seventeen, just a light-skinned simpering fool with her bit
lower lip and a way of ducking her chin when she looked at him. Of
course anyone might have suspected but she just seemed too flimsy,
the most forceful thing about her that navel ring and smooth flat belly.

WOULD YOU RATHER GET A PRICKER IN YOUR HEART OR YOUR HEEL? I saw
she had texted him one day, the first moment that made me suspicious.

Is Lucia texting you about prickers? I said.

Some kind of word game she likes playing, he said, holding my
gaze in the straightforward way that had passed him from jail to

parole board to clean man, containing enough sugar to make your average neighborhood vigilante for the defense of the revolution trust in Yuzniel.

Oh come on, I said, should I ask?

Look, the girl just lost her father, he said, you want me to turn a blind eye on her just because you're jealous?

What, I said, hotels? Or friends' places?

Yanet, don't go crazy too, he said, right when I need you. Jealous about a baby? You and I were just talking about having one ourselves.

You weren't ready.

But we're talking, right?

So I was just supposed to swallow this and go about my day, check on accounts, talk to all his smiling ex-cons and not care when of course I was beyond ready to have kids, already in my thirties with no solid person to confide in. The truth was our lives were so entwined I had no person who didn't think of Yuzniel as a personal savior, our neighborhood's hero. So I burned all day and on the next told him I wanted to relieve one of the ex-cons, work in the snack shop just to be sure coffee was being served correctly or some other ridiculous story. He took this as he took all my initiatives, calmly, eyeing me, calculating and then saying, as he so often did: You know best, Yanet. Let me know if I can help.

In the morning, he saw me in my apron in the snack bar while he was supposedly heading off to talk with his prepared-foods supplier in Central Havana, his little red Lada moving out into traffic, little knowing I had asked my cousin, my harelipped beloved cousin who drove a gypsy cab, to follow, a good choice of detective since my cousin's the rare sort to never be surprised by the faults of humans and is also no gossiper. About a half hour later, my cousin called before swooping back to pick me up, taking me to where he'd found Yuzniel, parked not outside the supplier's house where the smoke and carts press on you in the center of the city but instead near the breezy green Parque Almendares with its bridge. My cousin and I stopped on the upper rim of the park above where Yuzniel walked below, hands shoved in the back of his low jean pockets just like he used to do when we were sixteen, slumping down toward where they rent boats on the river that flows under the bridge.

We saw him look around, keen and quick before paying the guy who runs the boats—once, back when we were bad teens, he'd taken me here too. Ten cents to paddle a tin can upriver, nothing too cheap for that girl's torso I would have recognized anywhere, that flimsy seventeen-year-old leaning on him as she got onto the boat, making it rock before Yuzniel began rowing.

Well, said my cousin, palms opening wide. Your man's supplier?

My cousin has a one-up over most. What I mean is he knows exactly how people could break and still survive, and so his advice mattered. He weighed potential and disaster before answering. Play it, he said. Because Yuzniel's crafty, he'll admit to nothing.

I waited seven years!

Maybe that's your ticket? said my cousin, his wiles greater than I had supposed. He went on: Getting him to confess wouldn't be hard. But if you want him to stop seeing her—well, you know men.

This my cousin knew deeply, he the spawn of one of the Italian tourists and a young mother who never used funds sent her from a Milan bank for her son's lip operation but instead to secure a steadier income source, as she always said, one requiring greater long-term investment in high heels and lipstick.

It's awful, I said, I'd be that young too if—but this didn't make sense so I stopped.

In the end, my cousin showed mettle, saving the day or showing me what we were made of. He had our neighbor let Yuzniel know I had been detained. (Not technically a lie.) My cousin also sent my Y an unsigned typewritten letter, delivered by a beggar paid exactly fifty cents. In this letter, Yuzniel learned our leader's morality police had been surveying him. If he wanted to keep his business and apartment licenses, if he wanted to avoid appearing again before the dread bureau of moral affairs which could mean another citation and jail sentence, he'd have to sign a confession admitting to all his recent sins, bad as those of the worst American colonial mercenaries. Knowing truth remains the great revolutionary purgative, if the confession were done in the right spirit of autocritique, the parole board would be confirmed in its faith that Yuzniel had moral fiber enough to continue life as it was: however, his nefarious activities, moral or financial, would have to cease. By ten the next morning, at the front desk of the hotel nearest his snack bar, he should leave his confession in an envelope marked REVOLUTIONARY DOCUMENT. No one else could bring the letter, which, if written in ill faith, would warrant his return to prison.

You can imagine with what caught breath the next morning I leaned out of the window above the snack bar, where a loveseat may have witnessed some of Yuzniel's recent actions.

Did I love or hate him most during the moment I watched my boy totter with head lowered across the street and up the ramp to where the hotel guards nodded and let him pass through the glass doors? Who knows. I do know that the wind had never fluttered the hotel flags so beautifully and for the first time the palm trees looked splayed out, desperate for love. If I were a pop singer I could sing a story about the trees and flags, the guards and the letter that must have burnt a hole in Yuzniel's hands. I watched, sure that he and I could right everything, just the same way he had made good of the deck of cards he'd been dealt, his country, family, career, prison. He would figure this one out. On the other side, we would laugh together the way we had when we rode our high school wall.

I could hold it all in my hand, that little bird of what I saw we could have. Even if for some reason we hadn't had kids yet, the way most people did, maybe because of chemical water we drank as kids during the era in which you could light flames from the tap, I was not giving up hope. Our children would get Z names, Zuzu and Zamila and Zajuan, our new snack bar would boom, and we'd keep good stray kids off the street the way our parents had not.

Well, about half an hour later, my cousin came limping out of the hotel. Because of the mood swings among our Havana maintenance crews, only two weeks earlier the apartment above had crumbled into his and one of his legs worked slower than I remembered. From my upstairs window I tried reading the situation but could not and ran down the stairs. Of course who was coming upstairs but the one boy I had ever dreamed about, the one I still could not help seeing as a saint, the buddha of the Vedado as everyone called him, Yuzniel who didn't need much, who could grant others happiness?

Yanet, he said, softly, brushing my shoulders, and I might have realized the apelike message meant by this. Despite knowing he had lied to me, I could not understand what in the end turned out to be as much apology as a goodbye.

I do find myself unable to throw away the letter he left at the hotel. Because what trashcan is big enough to contain it?

Let it be known my dealings have been just as honest as the revolution. I have done nothing but what the system asked of me. As for the women in my life, the heart wants what it does. I cannot blame it for wanting a solicitous youth who might have been mine if unfortunate circumstances had not stolen a few years. Judge me but look in your own mirror and can you condemn?

I ask: Would you denounce such a man, or do you start with our leader or that slut? I see her in the hall smiling crocodile teeth, pregnant belly rounding her rainbow shirt, the curve of all we could have had if our great reforms had not thrown my boy in prison. And what this means is I lost the flower of my youth to a boy from Generation Y and all I got was some pay-off money, but as we were taught: never give up hope, venceremos siempre, and some better story could round my bend soon, especially since it happens I am next in line to be asked to come to Orlando by an uncle. And who can say the day I step off our beautiful isle will not be the exact day that the man to cause us such suffering will finally go to hell?

KNAVES

QUINCEAÑERA

Get out of this donut store where I'm the one responsible for dropping the dough into the vat of hot oil at five in the morning, making donuts and their holes and go all the way back to the night where nothing happened. Still you would come up with your hands empty. People like chalking up blame. When they do, I laugh. How could it all be my doing? This story really happened but that doesn't make it my fault.

First Monday of third grade, Lili arrived at our school. I spotted her older sister walking the halls but it took till Thursday for me to realize their connection, lined up for the bus looking carved by different knives.

Seeing Lili, you'd think she was round and cute like one of those dolls in an ad with too much echo that makes you know some welfare mom will buy it on sale, Lili's hair long, straight, and so shiny it could make you want to take a scissors to it, while her sister even in fifth grade had big hulking shoulders and a face that might as well have been pared jagged by one of our rusty blades in wood shop. Plus the nose on that face, like my mother said about people, the nose on that face—to me that nose was identical to the Indian statue outside our village cigar store, the one so exciting to our vandals the storeowner had to drag it inside every night.

Later I learned the sister's name was Ros, pronounced as if it should have been spelled Rose. If a letter went missing in the spelling of her name, she more than made up for it with her shoulders, meaty like a teenager's, two brown chicken fingers flat out her plain tank top where you could already see bra straps sticking out. Lining up for bus 31, ready to go home, I looked over at 30, trying to understand how the two sisters could be linked. This part I remember exactly, wearing my denim overall dress, shoved behind Emma, not listening to whatever she was saying about how Ella had a crush on Nolan and made him blush and how Tommy was always trying to stomp on her feet. Lili was the first girl I had ever seen who didn't know how to speak English and even if my mom liked calling me a smart aleck, I knew nothing about what it would be like to be that girl standing with her older sister.

Lili spent most of that first week in the front of the class sitting up straight as if Miss Connor could just hit some commando button to electrocute a student's seat. Later I learned number 30 went where no other bus did, tumbling on a dirt road at least a mile all the way up to some land owned by our main farmstand, the Portarella place. Lili's house anyway was in nothing you'd call a neighborhood, just one more trailer plopped among a clump of others strung with Christmas lights and chicken wire, all with tiny gardens out front and crooked trellises meant for cucumbers and violets, nothing hiding how temporary it all was, because even with all the electrical wire running around, you could tell it would take only a half day for that kind of home to be hitched up for somewhere else.

The first time I saw her place from the outside I thought it looked fun, like Lili would know as much as the workers who came each year to run shooting galleries and rides at the county fair, people who spent the week smoking outside trailers, spitting tobacco and jokes.

My mom always used to say I had a photographic memory. It would get me in trouble if my mouth didn't first, according to her, but I wasn't the one who called Lili a wetback. Emmett learned stuff from his older brother and taught us. Even if the same brother bullied Emmett till his eyes were purple, at least Emmett got phrases we all benefited from at some point and so back in second grade we knew to call certain boys four-eyes or retard, dork or faggot, just a sampling of Emmett's goods.

So when Emmett started calling Lili a wetback on her first day with us, when she barely spoke a word, it took us a while to understand. For a long time after, Lili kept reminding me how I stood up for her and how even on that first day she knew it would be me. Usually I never did anything like this but I did, I told Emmett to stop saying wetback because it made him sound special-ed, but then Dalton who really was special-ed said it just meant Lili was Mexican as a taco.

That part also wasn't true. An hour later, Miss Connor wanted to tell us more about Lili—no Y, she kept saying, as if to remind herself, Lili with two Is, isn't that interesting, class?—and kept saying Lili is from Gua-tay-ma-la, the name of her country. She made us all write the name down. Guataymala.

I turned around and made a face at Emmett and Dalton. See? I mouthed. Not Mexico!

So that was the first time I got in trouble because of Lili.

Because Miss Connor thought I was talking up in class, she grounded me on a chair sitting outside. I sat there, kicking my heels against the wall just loudly enough that someone inside might hear a code of protest while also thinking Guataymala could be a good name for a horse, one I would maybe one day have, like Sherry who took riding lessons, and I would sit tall on my horse and kick it to go faster.

That was Lili's first day with us, but on each of the next days, Lili relaxed a little, showing up with her shiny hair, sitting up straight, wearing the same too-fancy dress maybe three days in a row and then only one other. But she always smelled clean like she'd been scrubbed with Ivory soap, a fact I knew because her last name, Rodriguez, was just before mine, Rogers, and so I now waited to go out for recess standing behind her. And because things can be so random, or you can't predict how life goes, you could say that without the order of the alphabet, Lili and I wouldn't have gotten to be friends.

Once I leaned a little close just to inhale the goodness of her hair. I remember thinking as soon as she spoke more, maybe I would invite her over to play line tag one afternoon in the grass behind my house, the way I used to do with Emma. Because even in the beginning, every now and then Lili gave this shy smile which made me think she already knew English and was just pretending not to understand.

Before lunch every day, an aide came to take her out of class and lead her to some room where the Chinese boy Matthew and a Greek kid named Spyro got to have English lessons and lollipops, too, from what I saw. By Eastertime, Lili could say Easter and bunny and eggs as good as any of us, not a lot of words but enough. We'd also become friends. Not best friends, because for me being best friends meant you get to go to someone's house and eat chips without asking, you can flop down on the sofa and people ignore you like you're part of the family. I used to have that with Suzanne before her dad lost his job at the discount warehouse across the river and they had to move away in second grade. Lucky or not, Lili appeared during a lull. Before she came, and even for some time after, I was okay without a real best friend.

Even if it took my waiting till fifth grade to get to come over to her house, we were casual best friends. That meant we looked for each other at recess, we jumped rope or played line tag. And at the bus stop, I didn't care how her sister Ros always threw me a worried look when I said goodbye. As my dad used to say before he left, I had bigger fish to fry. By April, against us kids' advice, ignoring even that I'd banded my two kid brothers together to beg her different, there my mom was at home again, pregnant with a fifth kid.

She didn't care, she just went ahead and did stuff like this with whatever man she was seeing. The man's thing, the woman's—I knew about it all from what Emmett told us but who wants to think about their mom that way who mostly was just a person who came home sweat-stained and forgetting her hairnet was still on. She had started dropping hints about the manager from her job at the deli in the grocery store which meant when things got bad we got to pay with coupons and usually no one saw. My mom had her own issues, I could tell by how she started smoking again, telling me to go after school to the neighbor's, and also saying that once the baby showed up, I would think she was cute. So Ros giving me a weird look meant nothing until the day after my third kid brother was born when I was just hanging out in the neighbor's yard twirling the little thingamajig sign that shows a picture of a dog going poop and says CURB YOURSELF, the one still there. When the sisters came by, Lili tugged her sister over toward me and in her broken way told me they were walking to town.

By yourself?

The sister's English was worse than Lili's, but she nodded and said they were going to buy milk. Meel-ka. They didn't have anyone to drive them.

The neighbor wasn't watching so I made a choice and decided to go with them.

You do that? Go?

I shrugged, because it was not like I'd ever escaped before, but my homework was done and I had eaten the baloney-and-cheese sandwich the neighbor made. No one would notice.

Just for a bit, I said, the way my mom said whenever she walked out our door.

That day we had such an adventure. I don't want to go into it but it turned out I liked Ros too, because when she finally smiled, her whole cigar-store face became almost as bright as Lili's. I say almost because there was something sad about her and usually I didn't like sad kids especially if I couldn't tell where the sadness came from, and maybe I have it too now, since last year a man I hooked up with happened to say that the first time he saw me in the bar two towns down he could tell I had been neglected by my mother. Damaged goods? I said. I knew what I was getting into, he said. This was when we were first getting to know each other and ever since we broke up it's easy to remember how sweet the time was before my damage showed up to ruin it all or whatever. Twice he brought me bouquets. Once he said: I like the way you act like everything is such a big adventure. I only get now that he was some guy up from the city on a contract who saw me as some small-town hick with some convenient mounds to hump. At the time I thought, adventure, he likes my freshness, maybe he could even be the one, the guy. And he must have mistaken me for a different kind of person just because I happened to be carrying a yoga mat when we met. It wasn't even mine. But that's a whole nother story.

To stick to the point, after my first adventure with Lili and Ros that June day involving free ice cream and sneaking back in to our respective homes with no consequence, I knew I was in their family. Even if it took two more years before they let me come visit what they called home which was their tiny packed trailer.

People still like to tease me and say I was the one closest to Lili and I messed up her life but let them talk. I don't care what they think. Maybe next year I'll finally leave the donut shop, get out of here and go to the city. I'm pushing toward thirty and still think it's funny how of all the locals I always end up knowing city people more than anybody else does, because I meet them in our one café in town, the new place with the four-dollar crescent rolls. Maybe I'll go to a modeling or television agency because even if people say I have buckteeth, they can't help their small minds. Teeth you can fix. It's the other stuff that's harder, as I know from my whole history with my back.

One of the things we loved doing, Ros, Lili, and me, was modeling, pretending we were walking down a catwalk, using the stone walkway between my house and the neighbor's. We'd walk down the runway and swivel our hips pretty convincingly. The neighbor didn't mind, off watching television in her dark room off the kitchen, those boring soap operas where all they did was fight or kiss.

If it was the kind of day where the sidewalk was sizzling, we'd turn on her hose and play water games and call it our wet t-shirt contest without really knowing what we meant.

Sometimes I even invited the sisters over to have a cheese sandwich at the neighbor's because it was fun to trespass and all the neighbor cared about was that she got paid when she delivered me to my mother at six every night.

None of us lived the kind of life we saw on TV, which the sisters watched in Spanish at home as I later found out, but they also knew shows in English so we had that language in common. After I finally came to their trailer, I remember thinking Lili was as beautiful as one of those girls on their Spanish shows: one time, she was changing her shirt, facing her closet, the tiny one she shared with her sister, and for a second there was just her bare back and hair fallen to her waist over this sort of long gray house-skirt they wore, all of her pretty as Pocahontas. I don't know if the closet moment was the only second I wanted to be her but it counted as one. She called everything cute and nice, including the bunny in our classroom she wouldn't let go of when it was her turn to hold it, cradling it and singing rockabye, and then remembering to feed it hay even when it wasn't her turn. Plus her voice was so gentle, I loved hearing it coming down the hall toward me, I would get lit up after talking to her. That much I remember for sure.

So fast forward past all those elementary-school bunnies and our sidewalk modeling to eighth grade and the truth is that once we hit middle school me and Lili were no longer best friends, not the way we'd fallen into being around fourth grade or fifth when we'd sealed the deal. By eighth, Lili was speaking English good as any of us and was just one more in our pack. The truth is, I found it easier to hang around Ella. I'd go over when Ella wasn't at Brownies or in her 4-H Club, ballet class, or her violin lesson and we'd sneak into Ella's mom's dresses and parade around in front of her sisters and brothers and it felt good, like the kind of family I deserved, all of them reading one book together at night on their big unfake suede couch.

And whenever I went to Lili and Ros's trailer, which I still did, the only one of our group who knew where they lived, I would usually just see a bunch of frowning men in cowboy hats and jeans. Something about their bodies always looked too young for their heads and being around them made me also feel too hot and big. Too many people living in one small space, plus they always had different people coming in and out, some cousin who had just arrived or an aunt with a new baby. At Ella's house, you'd feel you had more space to move and talk, because in any of her many nooks you could just wait out any awkward moment. But at Lili's, we might as well have been in a bowling alley with balls smacking up against everything: two wrong inches to the left and you could become one of the pins.

Sometimes I'd be with the sisters slumped on the couch watching some show when their dad came home, a small tight man with a curlicue moustache and weirdly German name, angry as he hung his cowboy hat up after whatever dirty hacking and hauling he'd been doing in the Portarella fields. When he saw us three, he'd just grunt, already opening his beer by the time he got to the tiny fridge where Lili's mother always left him a plate of mushy tamales. He'd come throw his feet up on the card table and bark at someone to bring him something, a napkin or another drink, and we'd do all we could to scoot out. Mainly, at her house what I saw was this: two teenage girls, one bathroom, the mother and father, an aunt and her boyfriend and new baby, squeezed into a pellet of a trailer. The claustrophobia didn't mean I stopped coming over, especially because I liked the cooking of the mom, Lucia, who looked tired but had the girls' smile, and who barely half-listened when Lili told me how, back in their country, everyone around had been getting killed and Lucia and her husband had been just thirteen when they got across the border and to New York where they knew someone who had brought them up north to the Portarellas' farm. The family being so restless I thought I understood: like them, I knew I was meant for better.

...

But when Lili's fifteenth birthday started coming up, she and her sister started hinting about it during my fourteenth just like their party would go beyond even Sheryl Lansing's pool party at the end of the year in sixth grade. Like this would be the party to end all of them. I couldn't help being insulted because for my party I had worked hard, saved babysitting and carwash money and done other stuff I don't want to talk about and in the end no boys came to my fourteenth, not even Nolan or Henry or even Paxton, it was just Lili and Ros and our pack of girls looking at some stale dip, with crucial people like Sheryl not even bothering to explain why they didn't show up when I made a special point of inviting them.

So I was a little mad at the people who did show up, which doesn't make sense, I know, and then at my party the sisters started talking about Lili's fifteenth in front of me in our pack of girls like her birthday would be such a big deal? Everyone might have guessed I'd be big-time disappointed. I ended up picking the scabs on my knees on the back porch finally with only Ella keeping me company before her mom came and got her too in the middle of us gossiping about how Lili's mother worked cleaning people's houses.

I'd never heard Lucia say any English words other than how are you. Far as I knew she didn't work in the houses of anyone I knew personally. But before Lili's big fifteenth she was apparently going to take time off to start gluing little white bows onto pins, stuff like that, and needed the sisters, so after my birthday, each day the two of them left school with a big air of mystery and importance and also never asked me to come help.

Two years earlier, probably at the peak of our friendship, there had been an even bigger party for Ros but they hadn't invited too many people and anyway I'd been recovering, wearing a brace, one thing I don't really like to remember, my mom's work paying for the back operation which went bad, which meant any time I complained to my mom about anything, like about the twins being born, she'd say, yeah, and would you rather have your back still crooked?

Maybe it's enough to say it took me a couple of years to feel comfortable going out in public, and that was partly why my fourteenth birthday should have been a bigger deal while meanwhile Lili started to act like her party was going to end time.

As the day came closer, the sisters let slip to our group of friends little stories, like how Lili's mother Lucia had gone into debt, basically, selling off housecleaning services for the next year so they could pay for the party. That's human slavery! Ella said. And the dad who anyway worked long hours was working overtime and according to Lili was never home anymore.

So I couldn't help it, I started getting into the spirit of Lili's party, and maybe it was me who started this story going around but easily it could have been any of us that at Lili's party we were all going to go around in one of those big limousines a few of us had seen cruising around town, a long black submarine of a thing you could rent if you had enough money, and then Ros denied it, but the rumor had life and suddenly the girls could not have the party without a limousine.

For all the stories about my memory, one more thing my mom turns out to be wrong about, okay, maybe I partly started the chatter but when Lili heard it, my guess is that the sweet part of her, the part that could still sing lullabies to bunnies, didn't want to let any of us down, especially not the person who'd been her first friend. Because of me, she'd learned a ton. So really you can say it was more the sisters' fault since they were the first to start building up the party. When people came to our valley to get married, they always hired a limousine and the sisters started making it seem like the limo had always been a natural part of the plan.

The main thing is someone worked hard on Lili's parents to convince them, and maybe it was Ros coming to her aid like she always did, but who knows?

At school we heard dribs. At first the parents weren't even going to celebrate Lili because they had spent too much two years before on Ros, but that wouldn't be fair, I guess, or they couldn't bear Lili losing face or something was that important to their family.

So they were going to have the limo. And there was going to be a deejay, laser lights, fountains next to the cake. And Lili's dress— she was looking everywhere for the dress. She didn't want white, she wanted yellow and her hair curled. So what if I ended up renting a yellow dress and had curled hair too? Let me not get ahead of myself. Ella and I sometimes hung out with Lili and Ros to rehearse all the moments of the night, everything that might happen, and how can you blame us, our heads stuffed from the reality shows we liked, the shows about brides or whatever we watched on Ella's new mohair sofa.

The bummer was I'd have to wear the back brace to the party because, that fall, I still wasn't allowed to take it off. The brace, when everyone was going to be wearing the kind of thing we were all wearing around then? If you weren't strapless, at least a dress with one half coming off the shoulder. Finally I figured out a way to have one strap, too, like the rest of them, from the place where we rented dresses in town, and my curled hair would hide at least one part.

I could say lots here about the warm-up to the actual event but maybe I just want to skip ahead to the way each of us guests, the eight of us American girls who ended up with the migrant boys, got a little movie left in our lockers afterward, one part of the plan Ella and Ros and Lili and I cooked up.

The woman who filmed it was someone whose house was cleaned every week by Lili's mother. I hadn't paid much attention to her when we were all standing outside waiting to get into the limo at first. So it's too bad that in the movie, in the dark outside that veterans' hall they'd rented and tried to make a little less rinky-tink with balloons and streamers, you hear me talking about Lili and her dress, saying her yellow dress copied mine. Then you see me on camera asking Carol, another friend of ours who now has five babies of her own, to fix my back brace, pulling it up and adjusting it under my dress, fixing it under my hair. All that is captured forever.

And then you see us getting into that dark limo, all of us laughing. Those serious Spanish-speaking boys from our school had greased their hair back for the night but gave up their seriousness in that limo where we all got royally drunk on Jim Beam. We even ended up getting the driver, hired by the company, lost, not that he drank, just that we decided since we had wheels he should show us the gardens near the water that used to belong to the aristocrats who had summer houses plus the strip where old planes used to take off, the hulk of the chocolate factory, the river by the campus where all those badly dressed college students lived, everything else emptied and burnt down.

From inside the limo, our town looked different. We wanted to sniff it the way a bunny let out of the cage touches its nose to everything as if its nose is so clean and nice when really it was poking around in wet newspaper a second earlier. That night made us part of everything. Whatever happened later, I will never forget how every moment was a joke getting us toward something higher. Like I had predicted everything, how good it could be to be connected to Lili back when I got sent outside way back in third grade outside Miss Connor's class, back when I'd been sitting outside kicking my heels or playing with the Curb Yourself sign.

In the limo, like they had planned it, Lili looked like a yellow sun while Ros was beautiful like the moon with her dark-shadowed eyes and purple gown. The sisters and their mom had spent all those weeks making the tiny white flower brooches we were all wearing, and I felt that even with all our differences, who cared, like the song at the time said, the world was ours, we all had big open choices ahead.

At one point, I nudged Lili and was like: See, don't be mad about the limo, it was a good idea, right?

And whatever she might have thought, I knew she forgave me right then, her eyelashes so long and giving me the same tender face she showed the bunny. It's fine, she said.

You're having a good time, right?

I am, she said, though something in her eyes could have swallowed me.

Later that night Ros stood up and made a speech to her sister and Henry who was the only real nerdazoid invited tried to translate for me.

In English, Ros said to her sister: It's so great to have this party together and celebrate with our friends.

In Spanish, though, according to Henry, she said: We've been through a lot, the lows and highs, sister, things have been tough and it's not always easy for you or me, but trust me, it will get better soon.

She ended with something else in English, thanking the guests and all that.

After Ros's speech, her dad had a special dance with Lili, tugging her too close. I'd have been creeped out dancing with my dad in front of everyone like that, his hand resting on her waist while she did that little one-two swishing hip thing they always did. I was standing next to his old parents who had come all the way from their country. Lili's mother had cleaned enough houses to pay for their plane tickets, and I liked the grandfather, a tough old cowboy tearing up, waving away the photographer who got on him like a vulture before she took photos of the grandmother who was more of a backwoods peasant, acting as if she didn't know what century she had crawled into, just wearing one of those long gray trailer skirts and wringing her hands in front of her.

There was a lot of announcing in English and Spanish by the deejays, important moments, all that echo and boom I knew from the one bad Spanish radio station they had on in their trailer. Why do they all love echo so much? That's the least of my questions. Her parents presented her with a ring and then came the moment when Lili's little brother came to scatter rose petals with the mother from a basket. There was also the dance where a few boys from our school did some awkward steps with Ros, Lili, and two other girls from our pack. I wasn't mad I wasn't chosen, or maybe I was, but I figured it might have had something to do with the brace.

To distract myself I watched one woman dancing near the kitchen, by the cake with its fountains, someone shimmying more freely than any other woman in the place. If anyone spoke to her, she never stopped and just said: I love to dance! She kept adjusting her zebra strapless dress. I didn't get why she had no shame and everyone else was so much stiffer. Most other women seemed to have come down from the mountains like Lili's mother, mostly ignoring the single men who worked like Lili's father on some farm but who on that night sat under their cowboy hats at long tables with only their beer bottles for company. Behind everyone hung a big flag commemorating 9/11 which a lot of people used as backdrop for photos before they lined up for the food, foil trays of rice and beans, chicken, pork, and some kind of wilted iceberg lettuce with heavy ranch. I remember thinking: Is this what they serve at a fancy party? None of it went with Lili's dress, the cake fountain, any of it.

One of the boys told me we'd taken too long in the limo. The food wasn't supposed to come before Lili returned and there'd been a long period when we were getting the driver lost that everyone just sat at long tables under the streamers, the cowboy-hat men and their bottles waiting for us. Because the party started so late, the parents would have to pay everyone overtime.

Well, once the real party started, I wasn't the only one who had a good time. The lights went down, the lasers started flipping out, we all danced but the truth is I do remember feeling a little sick after the drink and bad food, plus my brace kept sticking out of my dress, at least as I saw it in the photos later. The week after I didn't care about any of that, more about what happened when someone started the rumor.

Girls at school whispered I had done it. Whatever made Lili push her mom so much to have such a big event: it all came from me. Not just the limo. The cake and dress, the whole bit. That at first the family wasn't even going to celebrate.

Me? I said, flipping my hair back. Why would Lili make me the one to decide? Hadn't she started talking to me about it? Hadn't she been so nice in the limo? Wasn't I one of the chosen who got to ride? But I was secretly flattered, even if that began a whole period when Lili and I didn't even talk to each other. Everything I know about her or what happened later came to me through others. Here's what I heard:

That after the dad took his old parents back to the airport, he got sad, thinking it was the last time he'd ever see them: he didn't have any documents. Because the laws changed after 9/11, he couldn't go back and see them, even though he had a kind of driver's license, and was the only one in the family who could drive the mom to cleaning jobs. Of all of them, the only legal one was baby Harold who'd just been born in the trailer. You see how none of this is my fault. So the dad was sad and then went down a bad spiral. He started getting mad about the girls going out. Two weeks after he'd danced with Lili, the girls went without permission to town for ice cream at Udder Heaven and, suspecting something, the dad came looking and caught them hanging out under the big wooden statue of the cow where he found them talking to boys, going against his rules and curfew and all. Supposedly you could smell the liquor. According to one of the friends, he was drunk later that night when he beat Ros with a paddle. I don't know if it was the first time or if it explains the way Ros started acting so sullen at school. As a junior she could have been practically a queen but I saw her like a dead puppet rehearsing with the others for the year's final show.

When the school counselor got suspicious and Ros still wouldn't talk, they called in Lili to explain. Lili was the one who got okay grades but Ros had always been kind of decent and now she wasn't. Alone with the counselor, Lili must have ratted her sister out enough for the court to order that the dad couldn't get five hundred feet close to his own trailer. He could only see his own kids if there was someone court-approved with him. Then a mean lady lawyer took the mom's case and started saying well, you could always divorce? Both the father and mother had to take time off from work to show up all round-eyed in court, this was the part I heard from Ella who had enough Spanish that she agreed to come once as a helper or witness for Lili in court. The girls had to sit alone together while the lawyers talked about their family and later they translated for their mom. They all had crushes on the lawyer for Lili and Ros because he was this really nice kind bearded guy, so different from the lawyer for the mother born Puerto Rican but who spoke bad Spanish and was always screaming at the mom, saying: I am doing this in your best interests!

Then their mother would just stare back, frozen. Family court was crazy, according to Ella. The girls' lawyer told them that any lawyer that manages to stay on has to have some kind of personality disorder because the place was the cesspool of the system, where everything broken came to stay. That's what it sounded like. Nothing ever happened. The mom and dad kept coming back and their case kept being delayed. Through it all Lili's mom stayed loyal to the dad, even when the court slapped him with two drunk-driving tickets. Two! I only have one so I know what this means, and lost my chance to even seal my record.

Here's the thing. Even before her party was when I started drinking a little, just stealing sips on the side whenever I could, whenever something was near and no one noticed. And so I was interested in the details they slapped on the dad, the rehab classes and anti-alcohol services he was supposed to get if he wanted to see his own kids. After the party was when I started thinking about my own dad again. Because usually I could just shelve thoughts of him away, but sometimes I liked to think of him like I did when I was a kid, seeing him as if he were a TV dad with a really intense side-part, a pilot flying overhead, always secretly keeping tabs on me but having sworn a vow he couldn't let anyone know.

After the last drunk ticket, Lili's dad fled before his court date. I tried hearing what I could, not because I was to blame, just wanting to get how everyone in the family could actually lie in court, saying they had no contact when they still talked every day on the phone and knew he was back in their country. The mom kept losing cleaning jobs because she couldn't understand the stuff of America. I'd heard from Lili that she grew up with a dirt-floor hut where they had a garden with their own beans and walked miles just to sell them in the market, just so they could buy other stuff, and plus that when it rained, her floor ran with mud. A girl named Hannah whose family had Lili's mom come clean sometimes told me she was no one's idea of a cleaner, that they let her keep coming because they liked her, but all the mom did was pile stuff on top of other stuff, sweeping everything into piles, mopping toward the corners, throwing stray coins inside the heirloom vases. Hannah said the mom could keep only about three loyal houses going which meant that even with government help they got because of the little brother who was not even a baby anymore, their family was barely scraping by.

During this whole period, I watched Lili from the corners of my eyes, not wanting her to know, because I knew people kept blaming me for all that was happening to their family. Not like I ever sat Lili down and said flat out that none of us are going to accept you if you don't have this huge party. Ella told me Lili was looking so tired because it turned out the dad didn't want anything to do with his own family, not just with the mom but with everyone, like he had given up on his American life, just left everyone to fend for themselves. Now the mom had no one to drive her around to houses she cleaned and had to take the loop bus, which was slow and came only two times a day. Plus she was so depressed, she had to find strength in her church. But the family couldn't even stay in their trailer, that miserable place to start with, if the dad wasn't working the farm. I mean, the Portarellas tried giving the mother a grace period, I knew because I sometimes babysat for one of the Portarella kids and overheard crucial details.

So one day the whole family, Lili, Ros, the mom, the little brother, all just skipped town and almost my life but not really. Because still the subject of Lili comes up with one of us. Say there's something happening with some Spanish pop star or someone comes into the donut shop where I make egg sandwiches for some of my little brothers and the early-morning workers I went to school with, and for whatever reason they get the itch to bring up the thing to stick me with like, hey, what do you think Lili is doing now?

And then they go on wondering or say how they had a crush on her but they always end by saying the thing which is that it was my fault, right, and I need to tell them it's not even funny anymore, not relevant. And they say something like how really if I hadn't pushed her to have that huge party none of her bad family stuff would have happened. And I say I don't want to hear it anymore. I don't tell them how sometimes it hits me too, remembering Lili's smile or how she rocked that bunny. Once an old crush of mine comes in the store and the topic comes up but I shush him until he gets annoyed and says I always like leaving things out. And I say, hey, don't you like donuts because the missing part is what makes it sweet? His eyes say I'm wrong so I say nothing, just serve him up his order in the wax paper bag and leave out the biggest truth, how blame can basically embalm you for life.

BEEF

We take advantage of that friendliness that Southerners are supposed to have, you know, the gentleman thing. What happens is I come up close to the door, press my nose up to the glass everyone has out here, and one of these people comes to the door, could be an old lady, could be a guy, doesn't matter, I start talking real fast, snowing it over them, which is why guys call me the Tongue, as in you want something, get the Tongue. Meat, beef, I've got a lot, I say, I'll give it to you, it hurts me, cost me three hundred but I'll give it to you for one hundred fifty, I'm almost shouting, *I'll give it to you*—and behind me the other guys are holding these black cardboard boxes we use and our van is puffing steam, our van also painted black, paint so thick we can't even use the rear lock and have to open it from the inside.

And if the people who open the door raise objections like: I don't have room in my freezer, I tell them, look, I've known freezers in my time and people don't know how to use them, no need to get namby-pamby on anyone, and I sort of shoulder it past them to the kitchen and start arranging things better, because one thing people don't know how to use is space and one American thing we know for sure is space.

I start shoving in the beef, packages of sirloin and T-bone and all that, racks and hamburger patties, and I'm opening up the box and hefting stuff in there, and if they say they want to keep the box in case of returns I tell them no worries, it's fine, I'll recycle, I've got everything flat before they say lickety and before they say split they find themselves whipping out a pen and writing out a checkaroo for one hundred and fifty buckarupees and if they don't, it's essentially highway robbery, because now we've got all our beef in their freezer, unpackaged, and possession is nine-tenths of the law, what can they do and anyway we're gone before they think better.

And hey, it's not like we're taking anything from them, they get to have beef for a month of Sundays, sauce it up anyway they like, some people would die to eat beef, and okay it's not that prissy stuff, none of that pure free-range cock-and-bull stuff, that grain-eating mushmush, this is real cow slaughter. We're talking choose your cut and take it between your jaws, bloody or barbecued or what have you.

This is what the lone cattle farmer has to do in our time. I mean, I'm not that guy but I'm hired by a guy who works with a guy who works with that guy, one local guy who'd never let me use his name but I feel for him, I do, and anyway when I got out of the hoosgaw after those domestic incidents what other jobs were open to me, I mean it wasn't like some national company was going to hire me to drive a brown truck delivering parcels or anyone would trust me decorating their cakes or whatever pissant job people find when they need to get by. If my mom weren't sick I wouldn't be doing this beef racket, because that's what it is, a racket, who we fooling here, but money is money and truth is, it's sort of fun, the choice of a house, the way you zero in like a detective, circling.

Trick is you look for markers that someone isn't really comfortable in his skin, like maybe you see someone with one of those cutesy mailboxes that show they're living out here because they think it's quaint, not someone throwing their trash out unbagged on their lawn but someone poking a rake at leaves as if he just the day before got introduced to the whole idea. Usually someone wearing jeans a little too tight. Once you're done spotting, don't move in right away, wait a while and come back in an hour, you have your guys with you, and the thing depends on speed which means that after a good take, inside the truck, you are high as kites, pure adrenaline without any guilt to tug it down, because after all didn't you just sell a decent product at decent markdown?

The only other job I've been able to get is working for the campaigns, I mean, at night, going around and removing signs the other guy has put up, people know me around here, in the electioneering scheme of things they don't call me Tongue, they call me Steam because I get away so fast, as in: you need a job done, you call Steam. Only the new people get shocked, usually Northerners drifted south because their cities have turned into habitats for rats living on one another, prime targets who don't understand the way we do things.

Just for the record, the way you collect election signs is you stack them on a corner at night and then come back an hour later. No one really notices. All these endeavors depend on patience. You got to wait that hour before you scoop up the other guy's signs and then go drive to the river and throw them in the water so that even if anyone dreams of using them, they would look waterlogged and who's going to vote for someone whose signs are mildewed? It's a message you should kick yourself out of the race, right? And the river's always better than going to the county dump, because any fool can dig up signs from the dump.

When I was in Basra I was called Steam for a whole nother reason. I was in Basra but back in Bentonville, where I lived for a little bit just out of high school, I had Cherilyn waiting for me. Cherilyn I'd met when she auditioned for the kind of place where bartenders dance and sing on top of the bar and she hadn't made it, they'd told her she was tops in the personality department but wouldn't help sales that much and so she was sitting curbside outside the bar, crying just before Friday happy hour, a girl whose cheeks were so fresh you felt you got the first bite out of an apple, if you know what I mean, while she felt I understood her troubles and why getting this bar job meant so much. All the other guys in my unit were jealous about Cherilyn, whose mom had gotten her wallet photo retouched so that no matter how many times I took it out of my kit, Cherilyn stayed one of the world's hot apples.

The bad thing happened two days before our little Basra Christmas and basically I was eating some turkey soup out of a can when we hear this explosion and everyone goes down, I mean even my can gets knocked out of my hand, all I have left is the spoon in my hand and that's the dumb luck of a survivor. The only guys who didn't buy the farm that second were me and the corporal about fifty yards away pulling down his pup. That one-night recon ended up some kind of life sentence because in the bargain I lost everybody but the corporal who was no big friend of mine though the moment did bond us, especially after we had to haul one of my buddies to the medevac that came too late because how can anyone get there in time to keep anything flowing?

The soup incident is why I got a purple heart, though it didn't take bravery on my part, just the dumb luck I have, the way they gave me a heart making up for all those other lost hearts, which is also why I got to see this head-shrink now because some wires got crossed, I mean who wouldn't need help? Like say you stared down the mouth of a nuclear reactor, wouldn't you think you could use a little help? Not everyone gets blown up and just has his stupid soup spoon left in his hands.

Which probably in a roundabout way explains how I got into the beef racket, the whole thing with my buddies and then Cherilyn walking out—we had a few incidents, cops called, all that, but really she walked because I didn't hang on her every word and mostly because she fell in love with some boy-toy prisoner friend of mine who only thought about lifting weights so he could update his photo on the prisoner website at the same time he was legally changing his name to Dream Big—all that just did a number on me, and when I got out for good, my friend Tony suggested I help him in a new business venture with guaranteed profit each month, he kept saying, right when I was ripe for anything guaranteed since prayer wasn't doing the trick and also it had gotten too depressing staying at home with ma all the time waiting for the veteran's check to thud in with all the other mail asking us to go buy things on the cheap. And I wasn't ready to start calling anyone Your Honor again. You can see why meat made sense.

So what happens is I've stocked the beef in someone's freezer and even got them to the point of sale, that's what it's about, you get them to use their pen and sign the check and put it in your hand and any objections they raise along the way you have all your answers ready like little soldiers, you keep saying, okay, I understand, just before you get yourself out the door. Vanished like the shine on Christmas decorations the day after the tree's down when it doesn't really matter if people hoped to get something they actually wanted.

This is not evil. If it were evil, I'd be a liar or someone would've stopped me already, because I'm not such a big guy, a fact I got reminded of a thousand times a day in the hoosgaw. It's just my bald head makes me look taller or tougher, I can't stop shaving it since I got home from Iraq, so though Cherilyn used to say I had super-kind eyes or at least did until the day she stopped, it's probably my eyes that draw them in and my shiny head what keeps people from slamming and locking the door in my face.

And you'd think that even after we leave they'd stop the check but they never do, probably stand a long while in the kitchen shaking their heads, trying to figure themselves out. Probably feel too foolish to want to explain it to Tanya at the bank, as in, Tanya, please stop my check because I just got taken in by the Beef Boys, the name we incorporated, the name we ask them to use, and Tanya wouldn't help them out either, being that Tanya understands everyone out here does what he's got to do. Especially because out here we got God country on our side, that's what we call it days when you see dads standing with sons around the back of a flatbed, unloading a two-hundred-pound deer hulk, everyone struck dumb by the fact that they get to live and hunt however they please.

People ask okay did something happen in Iraq that made you go into this line of business and usually I don't talk about the soup spoon moment, it's too much a tearjerker, so I can't think of anything else except about the next morning, which meant it was Christmas Eve when we were crossing this little bay which I won't name because it was supposed to be a no-fly zone but our fuel supply was low. We see this little action hero sort of gasping somewhere out in the water, and I was not myself that day, there with Johnny who'd been pressed into flight—though as corporal all he'd ever done was go to some military academy and get shipped out young, barely knew how to man a copter and so much younger than I was, a fact I never let him forget, but on this day I was trying to eject something out of my throat—I said let's go down, Johnny, that hero may be one of our men, which I didn't really think, but how can you explain days when you're not yourself?

Everyone has them, I'm good as the next guy. Still we get closer and I see the hero's not on our side, not at all, he has one of these superlong mullet beards, as we called them, a mullet what we called both the long bad haircut from all those 1970s bands and those trainers of young minds taught to battle us.

Like the guy might as well be one of their priests but something's hitting me, maybe because Christmas is the next day and we all should've been home two months prior or I don't know, I've gone soft on account of the soup spoon incident the day before. We scoop Mullet up in our copter and we're supposed to be heading to Basra to pick up some replenishment of medical supplies which have run low given our events, plus the fact that we've been bunkered in Bazookistan for two and a half months. And there Mullet is in the helicopter with us, spitting up water and smelling like something just dragged through major sewage, if you know what I mean, probably soiled all the way through.

The problem is he doesn't speak much English and the Arabic rattling in my head is not useful, stuff like *koos emuk*, which means *your mother's private parts!* And other choice words which I won't share because who knows why, but certain things stick better than all the *how are you*s and *please turn around and raise your hands over your head*s we had drilled in us for a day during pre-op. I can't help it, my head's not sorted for languages, but at least I remember one or two choice elements.

So the guy's gasping in our copter and I hit on something we could do for him to give him back some dignity, I go digging in my rucksack and I pull it out, it's a little mushed, but it's still okay, this hoagie like we used to call it back in training camp near Philly, and true the meat is mushed and drippy but still prime USDA, sent in a Hugs from Home package filled with diaper wipes and graham cookies when what most guys really want are magazines and beef, even when ladies and beef both come freeze-dried.

And the guy at first looks happy when he sees the puffy part of the bread, skinny as a bird and hungrier, because everyone understands basic human things as I've learned, whether it's hunger or self-defense, but he's saying something we can't understand, muttering a kind of question, so we're just smiling and saying *aiwa* and *lae* almost at the same time, yes and no, words even I can remember though neither of us in that moment remembers much else.

So what he does is take a bite and chew and it only takes him a half-second before he spits it out and says something which I think might be the word for infidels but could just as easily be the word for disgusting, and that does it, I mean I've had it, what with the soup thing with my buddies only the day before and here I am sharing my last KP with him when we have a three-hour flight at least to get to Basra, me with my blood sugar low and him with the nerve to spit food out because it's not cut to his liking or whatever because maybe the animal suffered and I'm all like who doesn't suffer and does that mean you reject someone's courtesy? I say not.

So I say: Let's drop him.

Just like that, let's drop him.

Plus the corporal doesn't even bat an eye, he's all like aye-aye sir, kind of roasting my bones because I'm a private but I don't care, he's with me on the dropping-Mullet idea. So we're over some compound, I can't tell what it is, one of their secret government installations that are everywhere on the maps like empty rectangles with squares jostling around inside, and we just do it, we force Mullet out, we drop him inside one of those cement blocks, maybe everyone has fled, maybe he gets locked inside, who knows, these guys can be super-crafty and have subterranean tunnels like moles. And Mullet can't believe we're doing it to him, I can still see his narrow longbeard face looking up right before we pull away, shielding his eyes from the wind of the copter blades but still shouting at us. Okay, so even after I say Mullet will figure out a way to escape because he has Allah on his side, the corporal seems too rattled to even crack a smile. When Mullet really deserved something, treating us with such inhospitality when there we were trying to rescue him, plus I shared my last sandwich and the best thing he could think to do was call us infidels?

Which is all kind of a tangent but maybe it explains why I got so bothered last Saturday when we came to this prissy kind of door, the kind with painted bird boxes in front of it, as if our birds here don't have any place to go find shelter, and the guy who shows up at the door shows me one of those concerned pasty Northern city-folk am-I-doing-it-right, still-a-foreigner-here faces. He actually has paint stripes on his clothes, so I figure he must be one of those gentleman artsy painters because there is no way in freezing buck county the guy is a house painter, or at least I for sure would never let him touch one of my walls, inside or outside.

His wife just vanishes like an aroma which means I see her white ankles disappearing up the stairs, probably out of fear of the evangelicals who run rampant in these parts and who you got to guard against because they'll talk your ear off for a million months of Sundays and never let you get down to business, almost putting our company out of business because now some people don't even answer their doors.

But this is one pasty-looking mother staring at me, and he starts trying to out-egg me, you know, talking some breed of stuff about how he doesn't need beef, doesn't even eat it, being one more of these blue-veined vegetarians starting to infest our land, and I'm smiling at him like I can't believe this, like whatever he does in bed would be nothing I'd ever want to even look at, I mean I'm not about to insult him since you never jinx sales, first thing you learn, because anyway I'm not in the intimidation racket, just into the speech-and-speed thing. Then he starts asking questions and for whatever reason it's not like I have good answers which means I'm starting to get a little pissy, things not going with the plan, and for whatever reason our copter comes back to me and when he says, what are you fighting about? I try not to lose it and say I'm not fighting, that was before, and when he asks, is the world black-and-white, I say, whatever you say, which is right when this painter smiles in some way that makes him seem twice as crazy. He starts taking the beef, just ripping open the packages and throwing beef onto these massive iron skillets he has, I'm not kidding, frying up our goods in his kitchen which is painted all these godforsaken colors, aqua or pumpkin or who knows, cooking it up, and I would've left but the guy's wife is quicker than she looked, she came back smiling herself, smelling of vanilla perfume but basically using surprise tactics that made this vet look bad, because she got me tied me to their kitchen chair with two extension cords which I can't undo. Must have had a brother in the Boy Scouts or what have you.

At this point I'm bellowing like a ram in heat and stomping all what out but who's going to hear me out here? No one. And she keeps interrupting her husband whose eyes could be those of a serial murderer to say, you're under citizen's arrest, but you want me to call 911?

You're not supposed to do this, I say, trying to calm everyone including myself. How it's supposed to go is you're supposed to let me free now. Right here you should be signing the check and—

And he says to her, not even paying attention to me: We'll just keep him here. The thing they used was surprise, which I'm still feeling embarrassed about given how you'd think basic training plus my

current line of work would have prepped me for better, but he's frying up the beef and I'm sitting there all tied and he's serving it to me,
not with sauce or anything, holding my nose to make me open my
mouth and at first I'm just spitting it out onto my lap or the floor,
and I'm thinking what kind of justice is this, me forced to eat my own
beef, but the more I spit the more he shoves it in so I figure better to
just start swallowing.

If it's so good, he's saying, you think we're rubes or something?
People you can just get something over on?

And I keep eating, it's okay, not raw or anything, not like desert
lizard-flesh I once had to eat, but I can see the Freez-R-Pak of meat
on his counter starting its melt, losing value as Tony would say, and
I can't tell which kills me more, the fried meat or the sight of fading
profit. My voice is weaker than I mean it to be when I say, Look, you
don't mind, would you please just get those packages in the freezer?

Because for everything I sell for one hundred and fifty, I've had
to shell out fifty, so if everything goes bad, I could sell it but I don't
want to get anyone sick with E. coli, that's not my business, I never
volunteered for nerve-gas patrol if you know what I mean. I just don't
want to lose money. I'm thinking of ma at home waiting for me to
bring her home a carton of cherry ice cream like I do whenever I
make a decent sale, and I'm almost about to explain but the guy's
talking too much, out-tonguing me. Meanwhile the guy's wife has
disappeared right when I sensed she could have been my only hope,
something about the way she knew to tie Scout knots.

Not to go on too long but it started to look like my guys had
vanished from outside, worse than steam, showing no loyalty, and
I'm sitting there about three hours telling by the folksy-cute kitchen
clock that cuckoos in the voice of every different kind of bird. Three
hours later, this crazy couple finally decides alright, enough, they're
going to untie me. They've made me eat the beef till I retch it up.
The guy even says back to me the thing I had said to him, which is
that possession is nine-tenths of the law. Being tied up had got me
confused and I'd started saying things out of sequence.

So that was yesterday. At least I got out with my pants on.

We have enough houses tucked away in the hills that I could be in business for a whole nother year before shifting to another line of work, and it would help ma with her cancer treatments, her stupid doctor who makes her exhale into a breathalyzer just to chart her lungs. None of it makes sense and nothing lasts forever, I tell ma whenever she complains but she sort of chucks me on the head and says, Jimmy you used to be decent, you were good at figures, you were quick in your head. I let her treat me like I'm six because she has gotten some marbles loose and there's no way I'm going to forget I'm all she has which explains why I'm so steady with the cherry ice cream except for yesterday.

Not to mention that she has reminded me it's us two alone together every day since my dad was locked away and me only eight allowed to see him once a month at visiting hours. Which is all a long way of saying I've been thinking and I've changed my tactics, I'm a reformed man. Which also means I see the world in a new way and look, you gave me your time, it hurts me but I'm just about ready to give it to you.

CATULLUS

Tell me it's not a tragedy humans lack whiskers but please don't take it personally.

You came for a wedding that turned into a funeral, I understand, I know all about funerals because look right here, a skeleton of my favorite, a tabby named Loti, she was the first with me when I came after the war, hanging right there next to that pile of dried fish. Which war we say now, which, because the people in charge are organizers who like arranging their little bloodbaths, their spills and mop-ups. So many wars but for me there is just the one that keeps going. That wasn't the reason I kept you on the landing for a while: it is just I so often get inspectors coming to steal my treasures. Of course I know about treasures. The people who understand best are usually bent from heaving a hoard in whatever satchel officials let you carry but look, it doesn't really matter which country I came from, you come from one, I another, and here we meet in a third. You knocked at my door, you say something bit your child and does any country ever really help? This is why I keep inspectors out of my home.

You might be the kind who might call whatever bit your kid a beast but it is not mine. This you must understand. Mine don't roam. They stay with me, twenty-two and each with no shortage of personality. Comfortable here, they enjoy it, and who wants anything different? When I used to read philosophy, I liked Catullus talking about the death of his mistress's sparrow that he wished he could bring back, a man who knew illusions make for dangerous enterprise. The more you think you save anyone, the more you destroy. That right there is the sum of what I learned from my education even if no one here knows this about me. Classical education but they just call me the cat lady. A little knowledge never hurts and trust me, no book taught me how to find whomever bit your child. At four o'clock, most of the company start to arrive behind this big block of human dwellings: I call it where the jungle starts. Like us, cats have teatime and they come sniffing right when dinner inside the buildings starts cooking. So come with me: you have to get down on your knees and sniff too, near the bushes. Do it right and they know you as one of them. Arch the lower part of your spine, angle your head to the side as if you can hear and smell from your heart. Imagine if we saw only one color of the rainbow: this is how narrow we are most of the time. Act as they do and then they'll show you their colors. Otherwise we need peepholes, but don't forget you can peek through branches. What our species has in too much weight, it lacks in imagination, toeholds, and tolerance. Look at a soldier's face in one of those moments you don't want to recall and then you know exactly what lacking imagination looks like. Your children might understand, acting so shy because one was bit. Humans call shyness common sense but you know a shy scent confuses most species. Surely your big one could account for herself more. You were all inside the apartment mourning your uncle who would have been happier if you'd gathered to remember him outside under the trees. Your girl went outside alone but must have been doing something wrong or you left something missing in her education. Treating another species right means waiting and too many of us lack the talent, the simple act of extending your hand and waiting. We lack patience and then raise our young to lack. I am not blaming you, but get humble on your knees right here in the dirt and they will come.

When I arrived here after the war, we found this place to live. All these years we have not moved. In the windy season, leaves fall and tell people which living beings matter most. Once the city became safer, I made my first friend with a Persian who had lost her tail. After that, she had babies and then others started bringing me babies to care for because they knew I cared like no one else, I would remember, I would keep even the skeletons safe.

You came for a wedding but your uncle was so happy to see you he died before your eyes? His wineglass flew out of his hand, his head snapped back. Of course he was lucky, dying surrounded by his family. One of the best ways is to have the heart stop in happiness, that action just as mechanical as the retraction of a claw. A full life that man had, so many grandbabies, a man who liked prowling from one house to another. I never entered your uncle's home, we never shared a meal, but we chatted politics on the sidewalk which is where he told me that a street in the capital has your last name, after his dead brother, and that, after a certain television program ended, he always pasted onto the screen this name of a war hero who died young defending the city: your uncle made sure to turn the name inward so modern-day announcers would still know this glory. That was your uncle, so thoughtful, the last on the block to remember the names of Loti and some of my other babies. You see I know your clan!

And now you still want to catch the one who bit your big child? You're the one with war on the mind. You want to quarantine the being for ten days and see if it dies of rabies, a terrible thing to do to someone breathing the same air as you. That someone should spend ten needless days in a box? Or spend its last days in that box? If it dies, only then will you give your child the shot? Now I think I have helped you enough. You cannot see the point in letting these babies roam free. Once these hills belonged to them, not any of us. I say, let your daughter have the shot already! And so what if a rabies shot could bring on delirium, hallucinations, nightmares, psychosis? Is reality so very different? But you can't help yourself, you are one of the others, just as hidden from yourself as the beast you think you will one day find.

I NEVER HAD ANY PROBLEM WITH YOU

I grew up thinking there had been a war, and that our soldiers
had gone to war to guarantee the democracy. And that there
were no disappeared people, that it was all a lie.
—Victoria Montenegro

Think about becoming a parent and you consider consequences. When you
came into our life, we knew we wanted to teach you the world. Even
now, we hold tight to the faith that this document I compose will
endure later history which has a reckless habit of making virgins out
of everyone, a tendency some call amnesia.

Never forget you represented such great hope for your mother
but since she died when you were young, she remains a memory
barely a shred beyond whatever photographs tell you. That said, who
among us can see fate? Consider antibodies' passage through a vein
and how we fail to feel such an all-important passage. Or how we
view stars, great and mighty yet appearing to us as mere pinpricks.
So much of our knowledge operates in this manner, tempting and
unreachable, usually irreproachable.

Did you know dung beetles navigate by the Milky Way? They
roll balls of dung before placing on their heads little dung-caps that

let them perceive the stars. So many things come down to a person trusting in similar rituals, in magnetism and gravity. Equipped, the beetles make their way as best they can.

From the beetles' perspective, their family rites make perfect sense. And of course it also makes sense, in eternal fashion, for the young to regard their parents with accusing antennae. It did not take Freud to invent this trick: generations increasingly turn on forebears with the rage of new life. To summon botany over biology, consider the unbent grass that uses the decomposed as mulch from which to derive greater vigor.

You are on your way toward becoming a mature young woman and are, moreover, with child, so I thought it important to hand you, our faculties still intact, a sense of what might be important as you become a parent yourself.

Once I had a lover. I hope this recollection does not embarrass you, now that you are of age, since what child fails to cringe at what an old fuddy-duddy does with his unit after the military dress has been retired, so to speak, a jolly roger brought forth mainly for special occasions, but I have always been proud of how you have conducted yourself, both as a student and at home, not to mention as a blossoming young woman, and hence believe I can speak honestly. Why? From early on, I knew you were a prodigy, most especially at the harp but in so many other domains: you a daughter whom I could press forward to my associates and have you read aloud particular words at one of the many parties your mother and I loved to have, parties filled with associates and colleagues—and what beautiful words those are, words that vibrate around a person enough so that he starts to exist all the more.

To you, our colleagues and associates may have been insects stretching forth long scratchy arms from one of our many over-stuffed armchairs, aiming to tug you close to their cobwebs—you told me once you hated the visuals of nose hair, the aromatic spoor of wet dog—but to us our colleagues were cherished company.

For them, and blame me for this still, I would sometimes press you to play the harp. You say now you winced as your wrists turned one arpeggio after another. Yet to me you had the face of an angel, always so good at reminding us of simpler times. When no harp was handy, to our colleagues, it is true, I might say: Ah, look what sophisticated words our daughter can read, how proficient she is. Often, it is true, I'd pick up a random book and there you would be, a shock to the system. You told me years later you hated this as well: how I made you feel like a performing monkey, but who would not be proud of an eight-year-old pronouncing such challenging words as *argillaceous*, your very first sign of being able to master an original difficulty, your voice carrying such strange and great authority? Your command surprised all of us.

Mellifluous. Autochthonic. Erumpent.

Your eyes flashed afterward, rating your audience. Since you could read any word from whatever technical book I happened to have handy, it is natural you wished to gauge whether we were worthy.

Were we? What I can tell you is that at a young age, you happened to be proficient. I do not share this merely to inflate your ego. Of course not! Nor do I preach speed for its own sake, the burden of the prodigy. Of what use is it to arrive at an end sooner than others? Are we not in trouble because so many leaders appreciate the expediency of future production as a way to avoid acknowledgment of the past? Nor should we disguise the fact that your mother and I were proud, I most especially, that you could take in the advanced ideas of the past and future at such a jejune age.

Of course later you blamed us for having encouraged you to skip a grade, swallowing time, as it were, but what were we supposed to do with you showing cleverness back in kindergarten? The teacher with the mole and slit skirts told me she often left the classroom with you in charge, reading to your fellow pupils. To that kind of child, what does the mundanity of first grade offer? You charge us for how you hold your pencil, never trained in banal cantilevering. And accused us for the meekness in your second-grade classroom that made you find it less embarrassing to sit in your seat and urinate, a small puddle spreading its shame, rather than leaving to sign your name outside the bathroom which both boys and girls used. That you were timid about signing your name stunned me. This was hardly a trait associated with my family line or the daughter I knew, the one with whom I now share so many fond memories, the one with whom I never had any trouble. How surprising then to learn that you carried your wet balled-up underwear back and forth in your satchel for weeks before stowing it in the back of some drawer marked *miscellaneous*, a word you pronounced with such lisping sweetness, a mark of your advancement.

But to return to the point, once I had a lover, before I was with your mother, of course, for all that your mother liked to say I was a great admirer of others, to which I ask are women not set down around us? Would you tell someone in a rose garden to close his eyes or at the seaside to stop breathing salt air? Everyone ends up with a particular menu of tastes. My own point here is that this lover to whom I refer liked me to slap her a bit and also to yank her hair once we were between the sheets. I suppose I should say when we made love, since your round belly shows you, too, have arrived at an unblushing stage, having disported with one of the young men with whom I have spied you, boys with such large Adam's apples it is clear you must have, as a girl growing up, appreciated one of your neighbors, one of those gangly boys for whom all energy collects at the throat.

To return to the point: I concur, making love is no blushing matter. Of course in my era we were idealists. In folk songs, girls and women were flirty but during our meetings so impossibly earnest, and how hard it was to understand these two aspects living together. Suture together a red-hot wriggly bonobo bottom to the bespectacled head of Karl Marx and you can imagine how we boys felt. If we rookie surgeons managed the suture, we enjoyed what came once we had executed enough healing on that pesky mind-body dialectic, making our subsequent wriggling a healthy part of the new philosophies with which we stuffed ourselves.

At such times, if one coupled with a flitty girl who turned out to be capable of earnest delivery, one felt oneself a lion of the nation, the loin of its future. If you didn't live through our times, this line of reasoning may be hard to understand. But our flutes and guitars, the fitful gyrating along with our chatter about the new world order, all of it served as a vine up toward the bedroom and let us know we helped a good system ascend toward its historically inevitable triumph. Not to linger on this point too much but say you were a man with full-blooded sympathies, it is natural that after you lay with enough Trotsky admirers, you knew you formed part of the national pride, so admirable and sporting. To any female you needed promise little, each a fertile seedbed into which you might bequeath the pearl of patrimony while also trusting no seedbed or pearl would betray our collective good faith, none of us thinking that one day we might have to become individuals all over again, knowing the pain of the adolescent forced to take matters into our own hands.

Of course, on the cusp of full masculinity, you can also imagine how hard it might have been for a young man like myself who already guessed what sacrificing to dedicated adult commitments might mean. Grow older and all branches become more singular. As if to become older means you start climbing an upside-down tree only to realize you now cling to one hefty trunk: the trunk has become your fate and only amor fati will be your limp consolation.

So imagine how I was, still early in my climbing, on one of the branches of that upside-down tree, still foolish in feeling this branch could lead anywhere, much as one begins a document like this, something particular to both writing and life: one begins thinking the branches could lead anywhere only to find oneself on the trunk of a particular conclusion. I climbed since I was an ambitious corporal, to be sure, and I had a lover, older than I was, more experienced, not that her flesh was any the less supple, only that her experience was so much greater that I wanted to plant a flag in it. And she, too, wanted me as a conqueror, this woman who liked me to do her like a dog. Does this seem a quaint notion, now that people are into, as they say, so many different sorts of acrobatics? She needed me to yank her hair back and then murmur words from our former dictator, the one from whom publicly we were happy to be free but who still ruled our bedrooms.

I do not mention this to make you wish to throw down this guide in disgust, though I begin to realize that this might not be a story I should follow to its logical conclusion. Again, it is merely that as a man of advancing years it has become incumbent upon me to share with you the wisdom I have collected, especially now that you might need some advice about parenting, one of the horrible new words to which my generation has had to accustom itself. We did not know about parenting, we just became whatever we were.

Suffice it to say, of course, as I rose in the ranks, aspects of my position became distasteful. It was announced to me, for one thing, that I had to leave the older lover in the dirt, without ever seeing her again: she never believed that such injunction came from directly above and not from my own distaste for anything farther below, in other words, her age reeking a bit too much of the grave. Paradoxically, soon after the discharge of my lover it happened, as a condition of my administrative role, that I came to be in charge of how people disported themselves between the sheets. Of course we didn't refer to the duty in this way. Rather, having ascended to a post in a cultured ministry, a post I had coveted, I found myself handling the question of nighttime behavior and was asked to come up with a new code of morals for the nation, something quick and slangy enough that people could recall it easily, something to use as a sort of dowsing rod when making a choice affecting our national hygiene, if you will, and so of course I said: Remember Our Traditions, since one of the first logos we had as a nation back when we were first forming ourselves in the more modern way was the man in his broad hat taking the woman by the waist, the woman in her peasant dress swung about. This man in his elegance, our fellow of the logo, looked as if he would have voiced our motto to sons preparing to leave for our factories and battlefields, heading out to storm the world, just as the woman, the mother of our nation, appeared with the cant of her head and outflung arm to have advised her daughters in similar fashion.

Remember our traditions. What those traditions were does not, in truth, need much plummy articulation: enough to invoke this glorious house of the past in which we were not merely peasants married to the dirt but rather gallant wielders of tradition.

And it is not just that this motto now appears on all our billboards and official correspondence, having been taken up with a spirit I could not have foreseen, even if there is that unfortunate resultant acronym, ROT, given the gothic cast the designer gave the first of each of the letters, so that we are ROTting away on every official communication and children see this ROT in their classrooms, but rather I see now that as a father I might tell you to follow this advice at least a bit more than you are presently: remember our traditions.

A few years ago you began asking in a manner I can only describe as querulous about some inconvenience you felt in the fact that we maintained no photo albums of you in your early years, in contrast to the tottering weight of those we amassed ever since you were three.

Every child feels the indignity of what a parent occludes, and what can I tell you, dear one? Your mother was a great one for amassing albums in general, to be sure. But what comes to mind is that you never asked about other items more relevant to your future, such as the case of Michael A., a man who showed the wrong kindness to a group of infidels in our government. What happened to poor Michael? He let dissidents dine at his table, his children play with theirs, and then one day, Michael failed to show up at his office. A hint of poisoned chicken was bandied about, a mention of foul play by a maid, and still one could find no trace of him, not the slightest whiff. What do you say about someone like this?

He was duped into his end, a smokescreen which, thanks to the protection of our family's tradition, you have never had to fear.

As I consider it, our troubles, yours and mine, began recently on the day when you looked at me strangely during an official lunch, when you sprang the question on me like one of the feral cats your child self so pitied: What if I had never been your father? What kind of thing was this to say as I was about to ascend to my magisterial functions, soon to walk up stairs that wiggled so inopportunely, up to the podium where I would place a ceremonial wreath around the neck of a popinjay, of course, a strutting man whom it was hard for me to celebrate, whose tail feathers have always been too hefty for the scatter of thoughts in his vain little head. It occasionally falls upon me, however, that I must celebrate the undeserving.

The opposite of such moments of unworthy celebration—and I could string a wreath with them—was always you. Do you know I could have had a birthday for you every day of every year we had together? Do you know all the times I held your head to my chest and stroked your hair? That I so painstakingly learned after your mother's death to use my brute thumbs braiding your fine girl's hair, no easy task for a man who, back in our darkest decade, had his hands hammered by unscrupulous interrogators?

How can you then turn to me and ask me such a question, at such an unwieldy moment?

Do you know it was your question that pushed me off my balance? I aimed for equanimity but tripped on those stairs, and as I looked over my shoulder, you seemed to be choking down a giggle, your face a mirror of what I saw in the popinjay's smirk.

The next day, as you know, not satisfied with public humiliation, you came upon me in the kitchen where I was having the maid make the kind of soup you once loved, the one we made whenever you were sick. The one for which I had to go to the local butcher's where he owes us some favors, his house having been passed over in many recent storms, for which he now bestows upon us massive bags of bones he promises come solely from grass-fed beasts of our plains, the bones with an architecture so large and misshapen, they are almost humanoid, truth be told, and now take up all the room in the freezer another fellow in our district gave us as a small gift at your last birthday.

Is it true—you dared ask, as I was showing the maid how to stir the soup from the inside of the pot out toward the rim—was my mother one of the journalists who criticized you?

The maid, an alley cat who speaks only the indigenous language, someone with whom I communicate in a pantomime, averted her eyes, sensing something disgraceful was transpiring.

I should have asked you a more serious question: Do you enjoy defiling the memory of your actual mother this way? Or rather, can you guess how many have been destroyed by rumor-spreading carrion lit upon the remains of our nation's hopes?

Do you know how deep my heart is? I asked before turning back to the maid.

The heart doesn't kidnap you, you said too quickly.

I have long believed every man has something to offer any scene of confrontation, yet it had not become clear to me what my donation might be.

I don't know what you mean, I finally said.

Love doesn't hide or hurt you, it doesn't lie to you all of your life, you said, love is something else.

Brush your hair! I tried, posture stiffening. We're going to be late.

You then went into a vile recounting, lies you saved up for such a moment, saying we had killed so many subversives we might have murdered journalists you mistakenly believe are your real parents.

You then pressed upon me a photo of two rebels you said you believed were your parents, given you by that awful friend of yours who likes to channel misinformation. How horrifying that you chose to believe such sources, when is it not ultimately a parent's job to instruct a child?

Real parents? I said, wishing instead that again I could hear you voicing with such sweetness those words from your past: *autochthonic. Erumpent.* We had that as a language, but what could I say back to you? *Popinjay, miscellaneous, virulence.* Mainly, I could not support any more vileness. I grabbed the soup ladle from the maid, gave the broth a determined stir and turned on you, my voice modulated to match our circumstances. You know, dear, I said, certain friends have given you the wrong ideas.

At which it would be charitable to say that you flounced out of the room, leaving me with the maid turned back to her pot, making one of those horrifying aboriginal gestures that could mean benediction, protection, or curse.

It was then natural for me to decide I could no longer stomach the official function to which we were meant to go and instead went to my room with its comforting morocco walls and gold-studded chairs, a room in which I could pore over a well-guarded black book, because of course there does exist one concerning you, its supporting documents neatly tabbed and placed in archival lamination. And so since one day you will find this secret black book, since I have not burnt it, an inhumane course of action, I thought it might behoove me to write you now, to help you understand some of the issues parents have.

For one thing, as any parenting book will say, the one I intended to write at the outset of this branching narrative, parents must work to contain the emotions, violent or otherwise, of their children. Hence it falls to me to gently correct your version of events. Were I to abstain from such repair, you would not qualify as my daughter and I could not claim to be your father.

To begin with, what you call kidnapping we call salvation, as in our saving a person from an unfortunate situation. What in your temporary blindness you call abusing power might also form a righting of collective wrongs. You might have had life in an orphanage, which then would have become your own upside-down tree trunk, all your possibilities narrowing, such little life cleaving to this trunk.

Instead I gave you our life. And yet can also recognize the beautiful flash of anger in your eyes, one which can lead to justice or truth. You are too young to know how rarely they coincide. This document, then, shares with you some of what you wish to know. You have not spoken to me since our conversation, believing it an admirable use of your life energies to keep smoldering. If you still think you should call those two people your parents, I am sorry, as I happen to think every person ends up in a cage of beliefs. Still your words return like an unwelcome report. Why is there no birth announcement, you kept on, eyes black voids, your hair so similar to my late wife, your face so much mine. The maid might as well have not been there in the room with us. As you leaned toward me, I was all that mattered to you. And if I loved you with great heat in that moment, with something I have never been able to conquer rising up, it changed nothing, especially how you smelled then, such a clammy, dank girl, my daughter a girl so much of the grave, I had to repress my revulsion, the only word emerging on my lips being the one that made you leave for good, one which marked your first triumph: *argillaceous*.

THE GOLDEN RULE; OR, I AM ONLY TRYING TO DO THE RIGHT THING

They like him because he makes jokes, singing old war songs whenever they have to do something embarrassing like clean his soiled rear, patting him down just as if he were a baby getting whatever mama failed to give him. He lets them keep their dignity and they let him keep his magic hands: this became the basic bargain, especially after the first nurse started to fly.

Because he has told them, they know that some seventy-six years earlier his mother asked him to lie in a cold Hungarian bed to warm bedsheets for her, that much he remembers, but there are a heap of other sentences into which he springs with a young man's joy only to end up tangled, sentences tying him into lexical knots and an aspirated gargle of politeness as if his listeners needed help in parsing basic concepts, as if they had gotten confused. You were saying—?

The person they are less sure what to do with is the wife, a tiny pert woman in a cherry tracksuit and a mostly upright derrière, all screaming her determination to cling to life and the forget-me-not possibility of dreamboats, her efficiency bespeaking the anxiety she has laid to rest like folded batwings in a closet before coming to check on how they're treating her spouse. To the home she comes riding in her energy-efficient touch-sensitive car, equipped with demands, one of those women whose life of self-privation means she is doomed to present the outside world with her impenetrable front which friendlier acquaintances call glow and enemies call selfishness.

Inside, the wife may have had some secret holy purpose, starving deep into the hollows of her cheekbones so she could be hungrier for exigencies, be a readier soldier when it came to fluttering in, indignant, her hummingbird voice and imperious manners ready to rally against all slights, imagined or not.

Be that as it may—here they borrow the husband's favorite phrase—they can't tell. They do know the wife has a habit of raising her voice, as if all nurses were, upon receipt of the N after R, deaf; and her main talent during her visits seems not tenderness but rather the asking of certain pointed questions about how well her husband's chart is being kept.

One nurse saw that on the application the wife, in her former occupation, served as coordinator of the county's social services. Some guessed they had on their hands a lady who had not achieved the status she imagined would be hers. Maybe on an unfrilled childhood bed she had twisted hair around fingers dreaming of winning elections, breaking important stories, being the first to split off from an immigrant family. Who knows. Maybe she had waltzed across a living room balancing books on her head. For some reason, she had to enunciate too clearly. With spouses, you could never tell. Could be that none of the woman's family had attended a lick of college, or that wherever her home was, forgotten, kept alive only by the umbilicus of the occasional birthday phone call, she may have had sisters themselves nurses, women who made her feel guilty for having fled the calling of service. For whatever reason, the woman they started calling the Hummingbird, which caught on right away, could never show respect, treating the nurses as little more than detritus on a planet on which she merely deigned set foot.

It could also be that the Hummingbird had gotten weighed down by degrees—you had to have a master's, at least, to head social services, right?—and maybe her knack for having been a good student, notating telephone conversations and keeping pen cartridges well-organized in drawers with little hole reinforcements and everything one needs in the pursuit of truth, having others tell her that she was important for so long, had slotted her into her own little crypt: you could take her pert requests as last gasps. Perhaps she too knew what it meant to feel stuck as any of the rest of them, caught in a niche, whether you called it nursing, grant writing or public administration, a life of private calibrations and collective holidays, because who can tell where a life goes?

Or maybe after each visit to the husband the hummingbird had to sneak into the wheelchair bathroom to relieve herself of some ache her husband had never fulfilled as she could not quit some habit of moving too fast.

Be that as it may, they knew the hummingbird had been prompt in admitting their patient to the home. I am trying to do the right thing, she kept saying. She and her grown children wore the sacred masks people find at the ready, the equivalent of old witch-doctor masks hanging in some basement, useful whenever someone has to stick a family member into what nurses called, never around a patient, the Crypt. Though the home was no more and no less than this: just one more place governed by the logic of financial realities, bedpans, germ control, efficiency, stray moments of humanity.

And of course there had been the golden era, back in the seventies, when nursing care was called the great cash cow, the graying of the population meaning the greening of pockets, when people with big ideas had checked in, boom years for nurses and speed degrees, for senior developments all over. In certain counties the homes grew fast as prisons after an election: to such homes you could lure people via tribal affiliations, Seventh-Day Adventist or Zionist, Anglophilic, Pastoral Ecological, or you could also offer them one-size-fits-all, because what did people really need in the end of their days beyond pleasant activities such as you find in any smart-minded Montessori classroom, along with counseling, titrated meds, and the company of others actively monitored for vital signs?

That golden age had passed. No longer was it the time when niches grew and quality slacked. Now in these dire times homes were forced to return to doldrum basics, old-time measures, ammonia and morphine, palliatives and hygiene, and even so, the husband's new place was known for its undrool factor, especially its pleasant activities, as the wife explained to her unsmiling grown children, the inventive depth and reach of such activities, not the usual macramé and bingo, the small-motor-skill development of basket-weaving but also—she flapped like a wing the brochure on which were listed wheelchair folk music nights, gambling parties based on thumb cockfights, and vessel gamesmanship, which was really, as one of the nurses had explained, a PR euphemism for bedpan croquet. His new home; no one could help the irony. Say we were cavemen, the wife asked her children, trying to make the question rhetorical, what would we do?

In the ninth century, in remote parts of the world, children were told to eat parents who outlived their usefulness, the geographer son with his undiagnosed Asperger's said, and then, sensing a faux pas, fell silent.

This particular home trapped members of the husband's tribe because it boasted reps of their faith on certain holidays, and gave clients the possibility of roommates who shared not just snore-space but ancestry. Because the wife's constitution prevented slowness, she barely talked it over with the somber children, each with a sticky relation to the father. Though the father had outwitted all actuarial odds imagined, though already ten years past the age of his own father who had died of an unjust dose of anesthetic during a minor operation in a far less litigious era, as the nurses would be told many times, their father was actually not so old.

To the children the wife listed reasons she could not keep him in her home anymore. First he had transgressed against her but no one talked of that, though the children fumbled hints, catching them or spinning them off into forgetful ether.

Secondly: the father had squandered money she in her public job had accrued, despite her attempts to squirrel it away year after year. He'd had one unsuccessful business venture after another, his gambler optimism and lofty-minded ideals no match for anyone's checkbook. No one talked directly of this either; instead, she said she had to hold onto what was legitimately hers, especially as she was no spring chicken, she said, straightening her spine, inadvertently appearing more like one.

Thirdly, you had to consider Virnella.

For years, the wife had enlisted the services of a maid named Virnella, a woman unhappy with the lot she found herself in given that her dreams would have had her be a film star living in a salmon-pink house with a curved grand staircase and children conveniently stowed in various corners, brought out clean-faced and docile to wear fancy fluffy dresses, accruing compliments as evidence of fertility, the children's elite comportment and looks thrown into the bargain. Instead, because the shadow of the bottle had crossed her household and she was gifted with canniness, she had to use her workable English to clean rich people's houses, sometimes able to bring her outwardly sullen, secretly joyous daughter to one of her houses, compliant about being stuck in front of television shows in which young girls shook their hair wild in dancing out the life the mother should have known, the one the daughter would, long after diabetes felled Virnella at the age of fifty, find herself seeking as a barmaid at Día de los Muertos, a country-themed bar along an interstate.

Years before any of that, Virnella's rebellion against her current situation took subtle forms, her mutiny a trickster coyote near the wife's speed. In every room V, as she was called, cleaned, she turned on a radio blasting a rhythm beating out the better reality in which tall men whispered entreaties, though sometimes she also liked the lubricious wheeze of the advice shows with their resonant boom. On Sunday mornings, she lay in bed with her daughter, watching soap operas, and when tears came, as they did whenever one particular televised wife was barred from fulfillment, her daughter would sneak V a glance, hungering to be let into the depths.

The daughter was named Nemesis because the mother had seen the word in that first doctor's office and it sounded pretty, only a joke on the first day of school and then forgotten until junior high, Nemi for short. If V made a few bad choices—her daughter's father being an alcoholic not unlike her own father whose fists she had escaped—she would set things on a better course. She saw where rich people sent their kids to school and was resourceful, advocating for Nemi with a Board of Ed secretary who thought it acceptable to wear curlers and slippers to work, so that her daughter got to attend school with those so privileged they had no clue about earning it.

And then one day a magic gift from God fell into V's lap, quite literally, on a crowded bus, a gem of a man with a soft voice and round face, a man from a higher class given his embarrassment in rising from her lap, all of which she found touching, a man who turned out to have riskier immigration status. Though she introduced him to her employers as her cousin, it soon became clear that Harold was her new beau, that one day they would marry and change his green-card status, and that he even liked playing father to Nemi, as he had lost his own son to palsy years ago: he was a good man, unafraid to plead with her when she turned cold, a man who appreciated that, in contrast to the lagabouts for whom he had fallen before, V worked. When Harold wasn't washing high-rise windows, he loved paging through self-help books: their favorite postcoital moments involved his coaching V about the direct way to achieve their dreams.

While the actual act V. loved almost more than any other material thing was arranging items of different sizes on a shelf, an act which gave her a control elusive in the general business of life. Tirelessly she arranged the Hummingbird's house, just as determined in trying to keep Nemesis safe during work hours from the roaming hands of her half-brothers. To the houses Nemi came, watched television, played with dolls, or just watched her mother's efforts with a blankness good at barring most inroads.

And the wife appreciated V's instincts, so that both women, going up and down stairs, had, on good days, a sense of lubricating a vast machine, sharing the workings of the house. Perfume bottles in a row, dishes stacked neatly, books arranged by height, satisfying to keen eyes. The nursing home employees later on were not the first to call the wife a bird. In high school, the wife had been known as a triller, and this avian spirit came over her often, humming tragic songs to herself, thinking of herself as a sparrowlike Piaf: as the wife and V worked together, she had the sense the two flew together within the world's economy of heartbreak, though she also chose not to know too much the details of V's past or prospects.

And because V was already with them for years when the husband started slipping, losing the ability to walk and then the ability to use the bathroom alone, right as his grandchildren were learning to walk and go potty, his throat thickening, soon to strip him of the ability to speak, long before he ended up in the nursing home, it proved easier for the wife to entrust the care of that slipping body to V., his body no longer one the wife wished to recognize.

And because there were also unmentionable, dearly held wrongs this same body had committed, V was a good stopgap measure, despite her lack of training as a caregiver, being strong and voluptuous, able to grip the husband as he started to forget how to walk the seventy steps to their house, perched on a dreamy hill facing the boats of the great river that led down to the greater city where V had first crossed the border.

It soon became logical that V and her man-friend Harold—whom she would marry as soon as they could execute a real wedding—took up residence in the basement, available now that the kids were gone. The pair stayed on call day and night for the husband, at a more than reasonable salary, because V knew the power of negotiation and also that the wife had the rich-person habit of having money pocketed away here and there. Taking over the husband's leaky bodily functions meant something magnificent needed to hemorrhage her way as well, a prize for her own future in which she was destined for more than the mere watching of telenovelas: she was meant for the life of the gilded neighbor with the curved banister.

As such, she and the bird entered a course of détente in which V brought her coffee each morning, one packet of artificial sugar with one sloop of skim milk. Good at keeping the house going while mostly ignoring the Post-it notes left her in big scrawled loopy script—V, PLEASE MAKE SALAD FOR LUNCH, THANKS—V showed brilliance in keeping the bird satisfied, and, when alone with the husband, V was not above holding his black-socked foot with affection, or, when toweling him off after his bath, slicking his hair back so he became a giant pink baby. In moments of fondness, she liked calling him her big pink doll. Be that as it may, he sobbed, thank you.

What V abhorred, however, was incontinence in the bed, and, given her lack of training, she kept her dislike overt. Every morning she found it fair to castigate her patient for his soiled sheets, every night chastising him as she placed his frail hips into a double diaper. All the other parts of the job she could handle with competence, smirking but her heart softening so that when he cried like a baby, she would say, Don't worry, señor, and even made a big poster her patient could look at, saying IF YOU NEED SOMETHING, CALL V, as reassuring to him as a map of Greenland would be to an armchair explorer.

Until the early dawn when her patient, in a fit of paranoid dementia, not in his clean pink-baby state but in his soiled dawn, at his most anxious and self-pitying, confused about which house he was in, propositioned her, saying point-blank that if V refused to make love with him, he would fire her. He took on the air of the boss he must have once been, especially since it probably had been years since he'd had congress with anyone.

Make love, he shouted before whimpering: Make love.

She ran downstairs crying, every detail shared with her smart boyfriend if just a bit burnished with a few details from the last soap opera.

Later V's calm, in explaining that unless her salary was upped by eighty percent she would not continue, inspired awe, stealing the wife's breath, making her heart gag her with a hellfire beat.

Once V finished her tale, the wife knew it was over: she could no longer keep the body and wandering spirit of this husband in a house she'd started to think of as solely hers. After all, who was responsible for its operations, its lights during the day and heat at night, the way it breathed, what it needed, its bill-paying and hedge-cutting, the minutest adjustments to keep up the home of their early marriage? Their home could not be squandered to this loss of dignity, strangulated calls in the early morning booming on the baby monitor next to where V slept in the apartment, the mentholated scent wafting through the house with its sick-joke potpourri, the ammonia bottles stacked ready in the closet, the poop stains on the Persian carpets, the shards of the husband all around while he himself made up a central gaping hole. All the wife could do to address that hole was call the children to her house. This time, unlike her earlier attempts to excise him from her heart, she would succeed. This would be no failed rocket launch à la 1960 in Cape Canaveral, a rocket combusting in midair before leaving the earth's atmosphere, this would form total eject.

Someone had told the wife, back in the early days of marriage, right after she had met her disapproving in-laws, that eccentricities get more pronounced as people age. She had used this maxim often, if unsuccessfully, to try forgiving certain people, but in the hours that stretched between V's story of the proposition and her announcing the husband's ejection to the children, she could not. She knew his to be no senior dementia: he suffered the natural consequence of a mind and hands that wandered all too much during the years of their marriage.

Maybe, the wife considered, the best proof for an afterlife exists in the brilliance and specificity a person shows in creating a living hell.

...

On entering the home, the husband did his best to charm all the nurses, successful with everyone but old Berta, canny at recognizing the loose-fingered ones. He'll put hands on you, Berta said right off, and since she had close to a 100 percent record in her initial assessments, most nurses did what they could to avoid being assigned his room.

Still, when they saw the new nurse, Letty, who'd gotten stuck with the assignment but who then came, afterward, literally flying down the hall, a movement in reverse started: everyone wanted his chart. He ask me lean close, then he kiss and grab, said Letty. I get quick out of room. Only then I fly, you say float.

No one could deny Letty's rapture, who then went down the hall to peek at the Groper sleeping, coming back calm and confirmed, speaking as if from a dream:

As small girl, I say one day I fly. You think he give other wishes, I let him do anything!

You sure his kiss was what made you fly? Berta asked, feeling the knot of cause versus correlation in her gut, hooking pointer fingers together to show her meaning, not ready to let the new girl get one over them so quickly.

Trust me, said Letty. Most of them wanted to, but then she also had the deep throatiness of someone who'd once had the virgin wink back at her from a cloth diaper.

Though few waited to hear what she had to say next. Skeptics disbelieved but already the quarreling was on. Letty could be bumped and so who would get to serve the Groper next?

Don't tell the doctors, they agreed, at least, we'll keep it among us. Because the husband couldn't have ten nurses tending to him, they took turns; and because he was unable to keep up with the rotating parade of faces popping in to change his diaper or guide him to the toilet or roll him back and forth to prevent bedsores, unaware of the havoc his ministry had caused on the floor, he just started calling all of his attendants Nurse, as in Nurse, may I please have, or Nurse, could you please—and would welcome whatever new face showed up to diagnose, soothe, or attend to the demands of his fallen body.

...

Over that first month, Berta's back pain healed, Mindy was overjoyed to have her husband give up the drink and check in, finally, to rehab while Sherrie was happy to lose her clumsiness. Inez lost her limp, Gloria had her workmen's comp claim go through, and Rosa's son paid a visit with her new grandson. At this point, some of the more mercenary on the staff were tempted to sell outsiders a grope with the geezer—imagine how it would look on the web! A subscription service!—but calmer voices prevailed, especially since some of the nurses had risen from their own versions of shady-lady pasts and knew a secret kept in the ranks was worth two hundred plus tax out in the world.

Still, nurses from other floors, getting wind, asked to sub at night just so they could serve the Groper, the secret healer of Ward 77 in the skilled nursing facility, because, even if there were no science to it, even if it seemed to work like astrology or aromatherapy, since you could not predict, fully, how or if or when it would work, they wanted to believe and all it really seemed to take was just letting yourself lean close.

They did find that whoever was on call following one of the Hummingbird's visits would *not* have her wish fulfilled, or if it was, the wish would be fulfilled in a tweaked way.

Applying scientific method, the frustrated ones started keeping a logbook so as to better study the pattern, and it became clear that it was wisest to avoid a grope post-Hummingbird: you just had to peek at the obvious links. Elsa's daughter announced, the day after the Hummingbird's visit, that, not content with just graduating school, she wanted to move away. When Joanne's new car came, it was a lemon that left her stranded by a depressing watering-hole on the interstate. Susie from two hours away had her bank account filled, by mistake, with someone else's massive deposit, equal to an entire year's salary, and after she bought them all burgers that day and said she would leave to study tango in Buenos Aires, the bank fees the following week left her poorer than before, though she didn't let it faze her, back to her usual resourceful self, heels clicking down the hall.

Of course, they kept the Groper's skills a secret from the Hummingbird. Yet on overhearing his new moniker, however affectionate the lilt, the Hummingbird misunderstood it, unable to keep herself from gloating: a sting of happiness to the idea that her husband was, fulfilling her worst prediction, corroding in a hell of his own devising. After all the Hummingbird had endured—the joke! Being called the Groper! He had basically lost his male organ and was now married to a catheter. You could not dream of greater recompense.

Despite the new age ideas she had long entertained about people creating their own sickness, she did not think to ask what might be her hell: she would eye a gossiping friend and fear the friend might lose her vocal cords. Or would watch her worrywart son and fear he would sprout brain tumors.

She decided to confide this idea that her husband had created his own hell with ingenuous specificity to her neighbor Donna, a hearty platinum-haired Italian married to her high school sweetheart, a person who used to let neighborhood kids run amok in her house.

New age hogwash, Donna said, just as the Hummingbird had feared: she already wanted to back away from the fence between their driveways. Donna kept on: Don't believe in some higher power, fine, but you think everyone creates their own realities? What about tsunami victims? War refugees? There's so much beyond our control.

I wasn't raised Catholic, said the Hummingbird.

You don't need to be Catholic. Trust me, if we could control our hells, we'd all be better people, she said, not making sense but pressing a sack of ginger cookies into the Hummingbird's hand before returning to what she loved, the great libidinal satisfaction of amassing supplies for her own beloved: scrapbook-making.

...

The first time the Hummingbird's husband had invaded her idea of loyalty, the wife had lectured him that all relationships are built from memory.

Now that on each visit he had less and less, she was proven bitterly right.

How are you? she always asked, giving him a quick peck while trying to avoid inhaling his mold and menthol.

She saw herself in his bifocals, swimming into a kind of focus. I have important theories on the flagellation of Christ, he might say. In my spare time, I'm redesigning the early aqueduct system of Budapest. A few times he was especially jolly: Goodbye, Nurse! he saluted her brightly, as if he expected her to fly off happy to be misrecognized.

Every week, nonetheless, the wife visited at least twice. As she rose in the elevator with other visitors, each coming out of love, curiosity, duty, or bearing an invisible flag of self-nobility, she would consider the place her man had ended up in, stuck in bed, laughed at by nurses. The Groper!

At some point in the visit, it would reach an end. Again she would purse her beaklike face into a kiss and lean down, giving that bony forehead a dry kiss and inhaling his odor, happy that in two minutes she could descend in the elevator and five minutes later could be out inhaling fresh air in greedy gulps.

Some three months into his stay at the home, one of the rare doctors anyone had ever sighted on the floor stopped in and breezily invited her to come into his office, a kind of closet next to the women's bathroom, behind where they usually kept the rolling mop cart. He was a big, bearish man, the kind she fancied in the years when her husband first started wandering, but she was too old, she was foolish, he had no eyes for her. He pretended to engage in deep study of the husband's chart and then took off his glasses, an act which he must have done lots of times with many wives. With professional, compassionate pacing he offered her this: the patient only had a few weeks of life.

How can you know such things?

I'm not God, but there are signs. Small ones. Nurses say he tugs at bedclothes. I just stepped in to see him. His eyes are glassy. His vital signs are okay, but when he sleeps, his breath stops for up to forty-five seconds. You of course have seen the rot creeping up his fingers?

She said nothing, knowing the rot to be the outward disease of her husband's groping soul, but believed the doctor in terms of the death sentence. Nothing could be deferred.

You know, he said, as if in consolation, your husband seems popular enough on the ward.

She felt her own heart stop, even as she said goodbye to the doctor, whose last name she immediately forgot, though it rhymed with Rimini, a place in which she had enjoyed her laughing honeymoon.

Immediately, and though she'd been looking forward to the descent in the elevator, she had to restitute matters. Feeling more like a hooked fish than a bird, she reeled back to her husband's room where she waited for a nurse to finish mopping up the path between the bed and the bathroom with ammonia. Finally alone with the man into whose sparkling eyes she had gazed just before betrothal, bright as if a crystal into which, if she peered long enough, she could discern such cheery potential, she sat in the chair next to the bed—usually she sat at the one next to his feet, but now she felt required to whisper—and waited before voicing her first sincere apology in their more than forty years of marriage: I've been cold.

He huffed back, rather fishlike himself. Had he not been able to make a coherent sentence only twenty minutes earlier? Maybe the pill he took to dry up the fluid filling his lungs wasn't working. Dosages had to be upped. Or maybe he was deep into a vision, this the term she preferred to hallucination: that much she continued to do for the husband's pride, never once calling him demented.

Perhaps he gasped something like: I love you too. All she knew was she had to lean close to hear him, as if he wished to tug her, small bones and all, into the grave. She was inhaling death: his muttering had turned to some unseen arena of private, attentive angels huddled close to his mouth.

Then he opened his eyes and looked straight at her, managing to speak more loudly, intelligibly enough that she could understand: Thank you for bringing me to this palace.

For a second, she looked for irony. Finding none, she knew how well she had consigned him to something he saw as heaven.

He looked up at her with a childish glee that just as quickly turned plaintive. Nurse, nurse—

She came closer, caught his hands, surprised she was choking.

What, darling?

A tenderness she had rarely used with him, ready for revelation.

Here they call me the Groper! he said, clear-minded.

I know, she murmured, using the voice she hadn't used with him for years, soft as tissue. Outside the door, for a second, she thought she glimpsed a nurse floating by, but surely this was because of the wetness filling her own eyes. There arose in her head the wish—perhaps the clearest in a life strewn with wishes—that she could again view the husband who might have been hers, the one she could have helped sustain, a man faithful and brave against all incursions.

They fight to serve me! he went on.

She lied: Good, because I was not sure about bringing you here— (this, when it had been one of the most resolute decisions of her life).

Be that—? he began, then voiced, loudly enough that she could hear, the three sweetest words in the English language: You were right! And just after, the two of them began what may as well have been their very first conversation, and if it failed to participate with the usual laws of both gravity and relationships, be that as it may, they found a way to start over.

MODERN PARABLES #1: THEFT

Don't worry, I didn't take all the soaps.

I didn't think you did, the older man says, searching.

Someone else might call the look the older man shoots his young comrade almost comical. In some version of later, the young man will tell his friends: Hey, but you should've seen his face. God I nailed him with the line about soap.

And much later the young man will say: It was a great ride, like the guy thought he was adopting me.

The message being that spirit will always trump vessel, art patron, and most stingingly, youth age. The artist had played lapdog to the rich and almost famous for a whirl, but now he'd say that period had ended, because he was to stay eminently unadoptable, untainted, meant for larger theft. This is what his listeners were meant to understand. The soap comment would nail coffins previously thought unnailable for the older man, whose name was Lew not Lou, because Lew retained a defunct era's reserve about Jewishness.

In the hotel room, the younger man shoulders his pack which may as well be a rock star's guitar, so great is the swagger.

A changing of shifts: the younger man has been put up here, at
no little expense, by Lew, who sees him as either a version of what
might have been or what might yet be attained. A splashy party having taken place the night before, not at a gallery but at a club filled
with shiny coatgirls and dark alcoves, dark coatgirls and shiny alcoves,
all the orchestration of the young man's career Lew has been design-
ing, maid service still to come to this one trashed room—but the
younger man has to head out. Head out, because the jostle of outside
streets will reward him more than shared breathing space with an
older man whose possessiveness starts to rub him wrong. The word
parasite, nebulously attaching itself to either of them, forms somewhere toward the back of the young man's cranium.

The younger man has made a career of kleptomania, which is why
the art world has celebrated him. You enter a show as a viewer and
don't notice when or how your pocket is picked. To achieve his ends,
the artist hires accomplices and distracting devices. Strobe lights,
sirens, smooth young talkers. At the end of the show you are always
free to swing by the front desk and pick up anything stolen from you,
though you're also free to choose signing the items over as a contri-
bution to the artist. Such potlatch has proven titillating enough. Lew
adopted the artist after having the German gold watch he bought for
himself at retirement, forever kept inside his vest pocket, lifted. Lew
chose to sign it over to the young artist, not guessing it would end
up forgotten in the top drawer of a bedside table inside some girl's
house. A person could be freed by such magic.

When the artist, whose self-given name is Maxx, was growing up
in one of those bar-flanked strips ninety minutes away from New
York City, as a child thinking the name of his town was Ninety
Minutes North, he used to justify his own high school acts of theft
as the work of a latter-day Robin Hood. He'd steal from one cloth-
ing store which had a corporate head famed for masturbation at
board meetings and attacking models. If kleptomania covered over
Maxx's mixed ability in paint, sculpture, or even doodling, well,

it took him a while to come to his schtick but once he did, age
seventeen, he dropped out. As he said on his blog: Manet couldn't
have predicted today but Manet—or was it Monet?—was blind, the
younger man not just making a joke for Lew when he had stumbled
over the names.

Maxx does have an endearing stutter that comes out under stress.
Also a sister who still lives upstate and though it has been a long while
since he had any real abode—last fixed place was boarding school,
later were admired in the press as a friend's sofa, apartment, villa—he
has told Lew he still belongs in some higher tree-flocked sphere, still
feeling meant to be another boy in a white shirt racing into Grand
Central to catch the 4:20 so he won't be the last in his dorm. A coed
boarding school—had any scene ever been riper for contentment? He
the black-cloaked outsider, the full-scholarship boy, there for artistic
promise, while the older man relishes this part of the boy's upbring-
ing because it didn't unrelate to his own boarding school experience,
single-sex because that's all that was around in Lew's time, the Jew
thing back then suppressible.

In his own version of later, Lew imagines telling his mayflower
wife, because he still has a wife with whom he reads the paper, attends
outings, shares a house: The boy doesn't know a thing about grati-
tude, who can blame him, it's his generation.

And his wife, suppressing irritation with this latest project,
another quest for meaning by a man with too much money for his
own good, a man seeking the grime of an artist who uses exotic
materials to make his work, because human feces and urine were
already so *done*, will harrumph, because she knows more than anyone about Lew's portraits on canvas, the nude figures and abstract
slashes, dust-covered and languishing in the unused drawing room
the way that Lew, who'd had something of a beginning, there in the
height of things, coming right at the end of the Cedar Bar but before
the hippies, is looking for something unworkable as a seahorse who
could live eternally, though all he gets is more like an insignia on
someone else's cloth napkin.

And despite his advanced age—or perhaps because of it—Lew keeps himself together, is still quite groomed, shaves every morning, naturally tall, hunkering over others in a leather bomber jacket that in all eras had the impeccable attribute of looking out-of-date.

It means something to him, the jacket, a steal on Bleecker Street before he'd come into his fund, back when he'd been young and playing poor, like kids of today, eating restaurant scraps thrown out the back door, affecting touches of poverty, living in the village and burning to depict the world they see. Back then he'd thought you could flame hot strokes across a canvas and others' understanding of the noumenal world would shift merely because he had lived. Later he would take lysergic acid and feel he conspired with nature to become the channel for all that was visionary, connected, and true.

And now here he was, living an outtake from a life he hadn't chosen, and at such moments he could feel the greatest self-contempt, following this youngster out of a hotel room, saying, *Wait! You forgot your other bag*, which was of course true, the younger man having thought he needed only one bag to achieve the effect of walking out on someone with disdain though after all the artist was no longer an adolescent, though he too would one day seek ways to be closer to fire, or might kill himself in the union of principles, reality with pleasure, after the puncture of his skin by one too many needles, the artist pushing twenty-five already—

—and from the bag the older man holds while chasing him down, hundreds of tiny soaps are already falling, one calligraphy-covered soap after another, you would almost call it the loveliest of tumbles there onto a faded argyle patch of hotel carpet in a city where even pigeons shriek in a pitch gone desperate.

DREAMERS

DOG'S JOURNEY

I.

Waves lack surface when you are weak, nothing risen quickly enough to keep you up, and keep pulling toward midpoint between both islands where you could be lost but must keep going like a brute force of nature despite the dwindled sap in your arms. If you never had faith, you find enough to say if this is what you have in store for me, either kill me this next moment or I will be your humble servant for the rest of my life, just strike me down now and let us not wait for jellyfish or sharks or else please stick by me and just let me get there.

II.

Other barefoot kids call you Bones because you are long and ropy and you are with them pressing your nose to the grill of the gym in your neighborhood after school. One day you ask the coach what it takes to train since you have seen him wrapping big kids' hands or ambling about spraying water into their mouths from a tumbler. The strangeness of such motherly gestures makes you think he may be that odd adult who doesn't bite, Jimenez with brows raised in the center as if the worst he has seen shocked him into generous surprise. When he asks how old you are and you say seven, he says your height qualifies you as eight and you get to start the next day.

No reason needed. All you did was ask. On the way to the gym, you kick a can because this is something you always do but two days later no longer need because you will not walk but instead rehearse positions that burn once you get there, the backstep and combinations while your mind stays sharp, this time one-two-two and the next one-shuffle-one, the bob and weave but also just the sheer joy of battering an object that could be anyone, you controlling the bag that loves you back, making you spark with focus. What Jimenez lends you is heart, your eyes fixed below the chin where his pulse throbs, the trick to make your gaze a tabletop no matter if he tests you by walking circles around barking the periphery!—a word which at first you think means throat, his a kinder growl than those you've known. Your knees bent, stance wide, and for a second no one can stop you even if on your first time trying a roundhouse, you knock yourself off center. The next lands square on his pad. When he is pleased, the corners of the mouth lift despite whatever invisible bulk tugs them down, the heaviness meaning someone like you comes once in a lifetime. Don't fall asleep looking at my face, he roars, eyes on the periphery! One day you stop hitting with your fourth and fifth knuckles though to use the second and third takes trust, but these will not wear out so quickly, he promises, dancing back before lunging over, holding the pads. Don't breathe not yet but slide forward, remember the sequence, double jab and cross, under, knees bent, duck and slide back, block, chin to chest, shoulders hunched, the way you should have been back when your father used to come at you. To punch Jimenez's pad is to swallow confusion. Sometimes he says jab through, give it more, but then says, what, you want to kill me? That middle ground dances away, hard to find the balance of warning that lives in his eyes. Don't look, he says, but can you help it? You make sure not to hurt this first man who shows caring, holding pads for you to thump but then taking a surprise jab. You must learn his way. Duck and learn. And the great curve of pleasure through your gut when the footwork falls and the pattern bursts, less about remembering to turn on this toe, no, the other, knee bent, and just about socking through like one of the old revolutionary songs they drove into you back in school.

At home your mother watches as if you have grown tentacles. Don't care. Slop meals into your gut before heading back to the gym. One, two, side, then curl, three, five, block. You've known the other kids in the place forever but if they used to be able to hurl the casual insult about your stringy legs, inside these walls you predict their moves three paces ahead. This one will throw an undercut, no, four, you disgrace no one but your vision sharpens. No need to wear a helmet like the older kids since a knowing pulses at the base of your palm, the one you stretch out after practice, unfurling the map of your future, a way out, bending your fingertips back toward your shoulders, making the intention of your mind and fist one. Less distance, get close, make it your game, Jimenez whispers, play it. Afterhours in that light slanted down late, you and the bag study the day. Punch back what you missed. Until you stop Jimenez will not either but there comes a point where his face thins and he sprays water into your mouth from the angled straw, making a step in jest as if to spray the little kids loyally covering your old spot outside, noses against the grill, shadow-boxing and spitting the way you never did since you were too awed to move, something big stilling you into being the last dog at the lair who then outlasts the rest, who knew Jimenez would never chase you off. Only now does he tell you to quit for the day, Jimenez seated on an overturned oil can to unwrap your hands while offering stories chewed out the corner of his mouth. Tactics of the greats. Hunger, he always says, quoting the great Dempsí. Sure, hunger, but no one gets fat on dreams, he says, confusing you. Which is better, hunger or dreams? He talks about aim and you cannot help looking at his nose, fallen with its massive sewn-up gorge on one side as if someone slid a machete out from putty. The nose and bloated knuckles, the first and second of his right hand puffed like a girl's breasts. My trophies, he calls them, one day you, he says, half-cuffing the side of your head. One day you will be his trophy. One day you study him the way you did back at the grill, the way he spits a pellet chaw of tobacco into the milk can nailed to the wall and he says terrible habit, follow my words, not my acts. Once the kids leave, behind them the yellow dogs clump at angles, those who love the stink of the place the way you do, a history of fluid soaked into split rubber mats and gloves but still what does Everlast mean? Jimenez also knows little English but he knows the one pair of Everlast in the gym goes to you, and you hang them on their rusted hook with dedication, in love like maybe the dogs who might think the stink of the gloves and mats come from one eternal, sweaty mother body. It must be Jimenez who names the children and dogs your first fans but after he does, whenever you see them, crouched or prone, you can't help some inner nod at their powers of recognition.

When your history teacher calls you to the head of your class, it is not to rap your raw knuckles because you cannot recall which white man had come to rape and plunder the virgin territory of the island nation but because at nine you are getting selected for some tournament not in your hometown but in the largest city near you. A royal mestizo, the teacher says, confusing you. While you have barely traveled beyond your town's own mountains, your little pueblito unknown even if Jimenez forms athletes who stream from their homes to haul glory to the nation. Apart from Jimenez, your town is mainly dust stretched short next to mountains from which cowboys ride out into the main street, along where the government took over families' tobacco farms, slicing them up and giving them back in pieces though mostly just swallowed, a town known for guavas and tobacco, not trophies and gloves, but the warmth of these becomes enough for you to wear your love openly. Probably you love your gloves too much, Jimenez tells you one day, his smack blasting onto your shoulders. Nothing wrong with love, he says, helping you up.

Mostly life makes sense in the gym, a place your mother calls the cathedral. In the gym, you take what is usually kept from you. Outside, Sundays at four you go to queue up for the fresh bread that will emerge from the government bakery, palming ten pesitos, and when you first approach the people sitting zigzag, no one's idea of a straight line, you say the words—the last? And the last person signals so you know now you are the last the way you will also signal to the next to arrive, the same way people try to leave the island, waiting for their Boca uncle or Tampa aunt to send for their escape, hoping to one day tell others they are behind them. Waiting, you pace, flipping coins in line for two hours, talking in the heat with kids whose mothers have sent them or watching grownups who lose their friendliness whenever they enter this waiting in which life stops. And no matter how long everyone has postponed anything else, once the bakery opens its door, always there arrive the adults who show up on magic gliding feet, free to cut to the head without waiting for anything, just picking up their bread. Perhaps it is in the bread line that the idea of abroad and escape bites hardest, because when the gliders skim off, some small murder clots in the face of those who stand and wait, one you understand since you've also seen it settling into your mother when your father hates the scent of her cooking, he can't help it, gas flame and onions do him wrong, all her damn ritual irritates, but when home and joyless, he bolts down her moros y cristianos. One day your older brothers and sisters are nowhere, leaving you and your mother plunged into the rites you like, she accepting your slump on the sofa. Your father gobbles behind you at the table before shoving his chair back, ready to head out after eating because he hates the stench of her cooking oil but instead of complaining and disappearing, he falls to his knees and then his face. You think he is joking, Papi, you call, and then your mother slaps him, calmer than you would think, all of this in two minutes? Three? He opens his eyes and comes back with a roar, cranky, telling you tranquila already, he has come back, he's fine, what's the fuss? Your mother flutters, suggesting possibilities, but your father says please no doctor, he trusts no one outside the family. He has seen the excellent doctors the revolution produced: no one has supplies and they improvise with cheap Chinese equipment they can't operate. Anyway, his was just a knockout! In the run-up to

the bad joke of this moment, these last few months he has rued your
new habits, forever reminding you he used to box for you to know he
did something more than be a ruined shell in the government system:
he wants you to know he still has a vein back to the man he once was,
entering a ring of equals, bare-chested, ready to swing. Later your
mother will regret having listened to him. I should've called for an
ambulance, she will say, leaning into your shoulder a little too hard.

The moment after returning to life, your father draws the drapes
before collapsing into the sofa to watch a government man intone
about the exciting new drilling the government will do off the Havana
shore, television light playing off his face, making him a statue, his
strangeness compelling you to jump rope in the apartment, part of
your training, legs crisscrossed and tricky, what your mother usually
forbids indoors but the rhythmic slap soothes, your stomach up in
your throat from the effort, meaning you almost don't notice your
father screwing his head around to look at you until you pause and
hear him apologize for the first time ever, saying: Sorry, mijo, sorry, I
am not going to make it. Then he passes out for good.

He didn't make it, the sorry echoing in you, only discipline
cleaning up that sorriness. Advantages flock. Your coach Jimenez
fills you with new stories. He tells you to stop eating bread so that
only two weeks after the funeral where your father lay waxy, you are
free, no longer waiting in the Sunday queue because your mother
and Jimenez talk for the first time after she finally makes her way
to the gym, wearing the mourning kerchief which made her look
tinier while Jimenez recites condolences and then with slow patience
the new litany: fish-head soup, beef nearly raw, root vegetables and
greens, avoid staples, rice, sweets, bread and butter. We'll try, your
mother says, our boy's skinny. But fast, Jimenez tells her, and a southpaw, which surprises everyone. Plus he's long but strong, like iron, we
should call him Hierro. She takes this in enough that she will never
again send for bread, you for the first time out of the queue, now a
man in the house. Only occasionally do you hear the ghostly heavy
tread of your father's feet on the broken linoleum. Two weeks in, your

future already tastes better. If your mother had never seemed happy around your father, after he is gone she sinks deep into herself and you start to feel Jimenez, who calls you Hierro, is the mother you might have had if seven kids and a dead husband had not tired your real one out. Your father, anyway, hardly counts as your mother's first death. You may be the seventh child but the sixth died before you were born and into that sadness you'd grown, the last but no one's runt, taller than even your oldest brother, taller than your father was, and maybe this tallness you half overhear whenever your tired mother and pretty lipsticked aunt discuss matters in the kitchen as they do now more frequently, half whiffs of bits, nothing you can locate. Far more understandable to spend hours in the gym, far more understandable the first time you fight a real opponent and hear a roar not because of a crowd but because you are going up against someone the coach from the capital has brought in, a rising star, a boy named Franco who has agreed to fight. The two older trainers watch you say hello to Franco as if watching their youth or a meteor shower: nothing for them to do at this point. Franco shows his toughness in not staring you down the way others from your town do, the cheapest tactic of fighting dogs, instead focusing only on his coach who stays busy trading stories with Jimenez about their shared time in the training camp. All this camaraderie sickens because you're partly meant to kill this boy, steadfast in watching his coach finally wrap his hand with gauze, your opponent treating it like a sacrament unlike the guys who glance around the second someone starts wrapping their hands as if anyone caring for them turns them into top-level bureaucrats and movie stars. Instead this kid glowers, making the smallest zone of his knuckles matter, the winding of the gauze as important as the fight to come, its first round about to make you forget everything your coach ever said, though once it starts somewhere in the back you hear Jimenez bellowing from the ropes something about the candle, which makes no sense when this boy hoves in, left hooks and cross-jabs out of nowhere, eyes tricky and hot, a boy from a world different from others. You cannot predict his moves but you bear down to find the opening, you almost see the candle, almost lure him into what Jimenez calls the house. Become the candle with the flickering head, that's all you try to do, the sting in your fists hungry to get him to his knees again, not wanting him to get up for a new round in which his fist goes for your jaw, your southpaw snapping. Trying to remember your own invented secret: to gain control, you breathe out when you pull back, no one having trained you, most people only complaining when someone toward the end of a match starts mouth-breathing and losing his guard, and though Jimenez schooled you in eight stages of mastery, the breath stays your own, a freedom making you bear down and absorb the roar. The fight could have gone otherwise but you end up leveling your first real challenger. Dignity is the first choice, you remember being drilled in school, and even if the great leader said it first, it stays your own.

Because here is the alternative: digging. Digging anywhere, in garbage cans next to piles of blond sleeping dogs to see if you can scrabble up metal to bring to the repair shop so they can patch cars and bikes. Or digging for favors like your neighbor on one of the government plantations where blistering sprays leave a person sick but still able to see a doctor at the hospital for free. Or for shelter like your father did in a government job where people argue all day, sharks snipping bits, complaining about tiny rations while trying to bribe everyone on the side. Or burrowing in to forget, becoming a man betting on dominos on the street while drinking cheap aguardiente. Forget digging, take a bus to the city to see what makes it run. Your brother Felipe followed that route and became one of the smartest drug dealers near the hotel with the best Internet, the one that brought foreign men looking for a place that doesn't mind them living it up with girls who then escape the island and send home packets of money. Felipe told you about it once he didn't have to leave the island to send home those packets. Then in an island-wide raid at dawn he got nabbed and spent eight years in prison boxing mousetraps. At this point your mother is tired out enough to trust Jimenez, the first outside man to take interest in her brood. You know only that the revolution broke his family into shards. Once they were one of the biggest plantation holders near your village which meant a few of his brothers got imprisoned for treason and bad capitalist thinking, one shot, one spoke a false confession for the radio, one fled for Miami, the last came back never the same. In this way, Jimenez learned revolutionary lessons, like you being a younger sibling knowing how to hide power and so good at counseling you in the same strategies. While you trust him because he found the god you never knew lived in your fists.

He must not be wholly wrong. Others find it too. Consider that first lunch, you already fourteen. A lady, the wife of an official who oversees one of the later tournaments, in the capital where maybe the great leader will also one day watch you fight. She asks what you would like to eat, her voice coming out from bowed lips under a perfumed cloud of hair, her shiver visible inside a shirt so thin shoulder bones nearly puncture the cloth. You realize she must not be that much older than you and shift in your seat as she orders plates to start coming: beans and rice, bread and custard, no fish-head soup but everything you want to swallow three times more quickly than she nibbles, your appetite massive, capable of gobbling the golden promise of her voice. In a week you will go live with boys at the camp to train for the elite team and this lady is the welcome sent your way by the government. Other than the mayor of your dusty town, she is the first government person you've met, you shuddering while her speech sings forth, so gentle you strain to hear it. Knowing that if you can just understand that voice, you will find your future made up of lunches, all will open.

What would you—and her cheeks flame, making your own cheeks blaze as if you are midmatch with an impossible hook landed. What would you—

—and whatever she says matters less than the wail inside, what Jimenez called Dempsí's hunger or the hollowness you know differently a week later when you're about to leave for the national training camp and Jimenez gets sick, hours before you are meant to take the bus to the sports commissioner in the capital and from there to the national camp, your coach collapsed not because you're leaving, you tell yourself over and over, it's just kidneys fail. Since it is a hospital accustomed to shocked people entering, you get to walk right in the front doors, numb all the way down a corridor of bad cases, their luck hard and your peeks horrified into rooms where all you see are yellowed feet and sagged flesh. Walking this corridor means sparring the nightmarish idea of Jimenez festering in this place as well as the choice of whether to turn back before you see him ruined. In the last room Jimenez lies, a tiny dirty box of a room holding a man who looks as if some viper has sucked all life spirit out. Because the room is tiny, because his cheeks fallen, he is too close for you to touch. Only a version of the smile you remember travels with difficulty across the mouth.

To look upon him so broken makes you need more than ever all he taught.

He was always the first to say he taught you to hold back your capital. Even if you were never supposed to use the word capital too loudly in public, except as a curse, Jimenez is no stranger to the obscenity, capital going through your head as you stand in the hospital, smelling the butter acid of urine. Which part do you touch when you want to run away? His right hand bulges in your grip, the nubs of those knuckles his very last trophy. No one speaks, your gut tight for the punch, this man both your ropes and mat. As usual he can read your mind and cracks out the truth in a dry voice: Seven years? meaning the time you trained together.

With the same tone he tells you not to worry, there is nothing you need say since once he had this exact thing, bad kidneys back in Angola while working as the leader's chauffeur, did you know, he was the one driving the national jeep. He survived working for the leader and so it follows he will outlive this. There could be no more useful lie, both of you nodding, but now he can't stop, telling you stuff that will not help, how he hadn't understood that war. Imagine the number it does on a man's head, to play foot soldier to a clown? As if this is meant to be a joke like the bread line, spittle bubbles in the corner of the same mouth that used to make you move like one happy puppet.

No one equipped you. You'll be okay, you say, imitating his lead and lying, knowing Jimenez won't batter this one down. Your gut dropped seven floors. Already you know everything but mainly how this is your first and hardest match. Jimenez tells you as much in his thin, splintered voice: You're good at holding back, he says, don't let them know what you're made of, hold something back so it stays your own. Maybe you'll get to America, he says, another dim quip.

You'll be fine, you say, blindly.

He reaches up, finger sliding along your stinging jaw. Just remember—

The breath? you say. At your code, he smiles and falls into his version of sleep, rattling out a goodbye. If you remained it would mean invading a face gone slack, only the slits bigger and smaller in that crushed monument of a nose. You stay to dab the drool coming out the mouth with your shirt and then leave, backward from a king all the way outside to the bus line where you say the usual phrase with whatever you can muster: The last? Forced to remember how in that hospital Jimenez said if you weren't already such a star, he would've asked you to stay to run his gym. You had wanted to say, yes, please, for you I'd do anything for you. He'd thought this answer along with you but then forbade the possibility, calling you his son, telling you to get off to the city already because he had another old friend, the tobacconist, who'd run the place. But then motioned for you to take an envelope. Once you stand in the bus line, you finger the spare key inside. And cannot go straight home so instead at the door, you try the key, making you realize all these years you never entered without your coach. A place so generous with welcome now looks injured, even the peeled-paint grill where you began. What sucks your heart out is you cannot spar with any of it, the body bag and all the equipment like bellies bursting with scuffed legs and arms, all of it making you pace, your step creaking the unlucky mats. This becomes the first place you have your own first crack, because your feet, until then in shoes you'd found the month before in a rummage bin at the government market, navy with only one hole in the toe, become no feet, only shins: you have lost your feet.

And on these stumps (the ones you find again the day you try getting one dry foot onto American soil) you run all the way home to find yourself tumbling like a heavyweight onto the couch where your mother flaps over you. Afterward, you have moros y cristianos and her sugared coffee as a going-away treat, the meal meant to betray Jimenez and his own disloyalties, hope swallowed just like that, and though after the meal you are sated and your feet are back, or enough to take you to the capital, one day you will land sputtering saltwater into the future ignoring you, the one that bit you back in the breadline, the one nobody armed you to imagine, which is the future which Dempsí got all wrong, since Dempsí was the one who called it hunger, not rage.

III.

Ten years of tile-laying. The good homes are those where owners bother offering you a glass of water while the bad ones have people who barely nod. To them you're just another dark head speaking broken English and they're paying illegally so best be quick. In the ring we called it the speed slide, off the ring. But try for a knockout in round one and it means sometimes your energy does not act like Everlast.

At least I work with friends, standing outside in the morning at La Floridita while cars rush by, the bunch of us happy lingering over coffee and croquetas, and maybe it was for these coffee friends that I came, or my girl and her mother, but no one knows why I make excuses and never bring family whenever I get invited to dinner at an American's house. Mostly I don't want Americans to know how bad off we are: they seem to lack some capacity for basic truth. Instead I iron my best shirt whenever I go over to eat their unsalty food, taking care of myself and also never blaming anyone for anything that happened. I'm the clean one who gets invited places. One of my bosses loves showing me his Florida room with its low ceiling and three dark walls opening up to the swimming pool. I can't suss any of it out: how does a citizen get from where I stand to where my boss is with his Florida room but maybe where I come from is what tears open my pockets.

Sometimes at the bar, too, people raise a glass to me, people I don't know who remember when our leader was on a rampage, who believed when he called me the greatest amateur boxer in all Cuban history until I chose to leave the island and became a traitor, what he called in the papers The Day Iron Lost Its Strength. Because the leader made his rampage so public, I changed my name back from Hierro to Icaro, my birthname, just another story for all of them back on the island, my mother in pain having called me the name of the dead son just before, this just another story like the match that never happened between our homegrown Stevenson before he became a drunk and refused fighting the great Ali, the one they always retell using the words of Che's goodbye letter to Fidel, among all the other stories we memorized in school. The goodbye story I want to tell everyone is different. Something to get them off the idea that my name means the great young boxer who swam away to become a Judas and traitor, a shame to the nation, the boxer who was the leader's sport for a few months, my case getting coverage with no way to spit anything back, my mother under surveillance twenty-four hours a day, punished for the escape she never guessed I would make. Back then, people liked calling me the crown jewel of the leader's system, the great mestizo: they said I had thrown away my royalty by swimming toward capital.

Here in Miami the biggest story does happen to be green. As one promoter said right before I lost that crucial match and he dumped me, here football, baseball, and basketball matter more, plus Florida money is too white, boxers black: in New York they support Puerto Ricans and Dominicans, in California they support Mexicans, but here you have the American nightmare, the way it is, sorry, son, and too much sorry son can make a person start to feel foolish.

At lunchtime I go to a little hole of a place on Eighth Street where we have one riqueño joining us, the food islands of grease waiting for any drunkard to think it a good side dish for the all-you-can-eat bread and butter, but nothing matters since a long time ago I gave up the training, not eating fish-head soup and running three miles before six in the morning. Here the coffee makes me buzz as if I'm getting ready before a great fight, the bread like the calm of right after, the cigars making up our afterparty, my coworkers laughing too hard at their own jokes, snaggletoothed, but what else does a new American need?

When I was eight I helped my father haul bags of sugar cane, his unjoke being that he was good for the national company because West African traders chose his great-grandpa for strength. In his time, my father was The Ox, part of why he didn't like my skinniness, the time when all kids called me Bones, before the system discovered me and I vaulted past him, reflexes my best part. Maybe Jimenez was right in calling me born to box, but tell me any greater camaraderie exists on this earth than eight day laborers in a sunny dive on Calle Ocho, smoking at one in the afternoon, most with at least one beer fizzing, television blaring nonstop videos of Latinas with the faces evangelists love to recruit, girls dancing half-naked with ribbons, our place with a name we'd know blind: The Miami Dream.

What happened during the fight I lost, people sometimes ask. I was fighting an Irishman from Chicago, the reigning champ, and so what if people later criticized me and said I was boring, like a spider in the web, I had my reasons. Come out of Cuba and you can't help being a technical, inside boxer. Here, in the pros, they want you to push your weight out of your comfort zone. My trainer had me tracing parallelograms on the mat until round six when I went American and knocked the guy out. Even more American in how I strolled the ring with fists up before the last count was struck because when you act like triumph is inevitable, do as Americans do, beat your chest like a happy ape, you claim the match. But then the guy gets up in the last seconds. This throws me and he's the one knocks me out. Did I make a mistake thinking I had a sure bet? And the contract the banker had with me was that if I lost even one fight, he could cut me, though if I'd started getting big, the banker would have had first option. So here I am, cut, past when any promoter would take me seriously, just laying tile and having coffee, my name Icaro on my American passport. Things could be worse.

There is a joke that people like to tell around here and it goes like this: The Cuban dog swims over and lands in Miami where the American dog greets him with a big lick. The Cuban dog complains to the American dog: I am so hungry.

The American dog says, Well, hombre, you got to get a job so you get money to eat.

The Cuban dog says, Fine, but I am too sick from all the bad water I drank coming over.

The American dog smiles. Here you got to pay the doctor, you got to get a job.

The Cuban doesn't understand. But how can I if I'm sick?

The American dog gets fed up and says: Look, if you want to complain, why'd you bother leaving Cuba?

The Cuban: Because at least here I can bark.

And that much is true, at least I'm here, barking, Bones with dreams once so big on a map none of us have the guts to pinpoint them anymore.

KOI

A small girl stretches her hand over the splintering rail, throwing food pellets into the water in a peacock-tail burst. Her older friend, daughter of the college's custodian, knows to savor. You can see her thinking: save up, throw one pellet at a time, wait before throwing the next.

To fish, only the eternity of appetite matters. Below the rickety platform, a ravenous will to power provides strategies to match. You leap over others' backs to get to any pellet still floating above the mêlée. Small fish circle at the iris, sharp gold zigzags, while a larger fish stabs in, its mouth an O so stretched a smaller one accidentally enters.

That's how Jonah got swallowed? the small one asks but the older one, Shanya, just shakes her head.

The food comes from a cracked twenty-five-cents-a-turn gumball dispenser placed on the platform, here behind the flower nursery, a whimsical convenience for those with time and pleasure-seeking on their hands, those driving past the college, the pick-your-own apple farm and raspberries and tannin stink of the winery to arrive at this rickety destination for those gratified by the craving of some hundred fish.

In a long-ago season, winter, the koi went torpid, sleeping under the black caul of ice, waiting to spring back once it thaws, a fact the older girl finds easy to believe, palming and warming her two quarters back into life.

After the koi expedition, led by Pint's mother—Pint the younger girl's nickname, granted by Shanya—they go to the goat-feeding place.

This semester, Pint lives in a faculty apartment near the supply office where Shanya's father works. Sunday afternoons, Pint and her mother kept seeing the older girl on a stone wall, nothing in hand, smiling out as college students passed. In this way, the friendship in parallel pursuit of fun had begun, Pint's mother saying: Let's go over—she looks nice, doesn't she?—bring a ball, ask if she wants to play.

Shanya is four years older than Pint, yet another carefully ignored difference; Shanya just eight, Pint four. Pint's mother aims for bridging, though this question between children of who was born first stays pesky no matter the adult smoothing.

Only recently Pint had come with her parents to live on campus, parents latecomers to the act, surprised out of self-absorption by messy responsibility. Pint is also startled, in her four-year-old way, by the self-absorption of the college students who don't notice her antics in the dining hall—hammy faces, eyebrows up, eyes sanpakku as Japanese warriors say, whites showing beneath pupils, cherub face turned into a tetragonal Halloween mask. Long ago a grandmother had cooed: She'll go into theater, a regular Shirley Temple! The college students are too busy losing themselves in desperate restoration of childhood, prone to riding on swings and odd embraces, pulling some girl off her feet, shrieking eros, the pleasure of autoconsumption. Or else they walk about like gifted harbingers of apocalypse, lone cartographers of the poles, sullen with wires in ears connecting them to thanatos, fame, truer audiences. Sometimes Pint wants to imitate them. And sometimes Pint and her mother go through a cloud of smokers and Pint waves her hand in front of her face: It's bad, Mommy, she reports solemnly, tell them they'll live younger if they smoke!

After the koi, Shanya and Pint and her mother drive a half mile down to the place where you also slot in quarters in order to feed the goats.

But as the girls kneel there, prayerful, the goats refuse to come. Too jaded, knowing the girls lack pellets, the little dispenser holding just crumbs. Let's call them? the mother suggests, the girls calling out random names: Nannygoat! Wizard! Kittycat! Billygoat! Cued by one, miraculously the beasts run toward them. Even the goats seem to find it funny. As if in celebration of a thing being called by its name, the big pregnant mama-goat butts her head against the chain link fence, her teeth pulling the zipper to open Shanya's little pink purse which protects her cellphone, the connection to her father, before backing off.

The girls enterprise. Avoiding grass, handing clover over to the goats' greedy nuzzles, which goes over big, Shanya especially gentle but forgetting to keep her hand flat. When she gets a little nip, Pint kisses her friend's hand and says: If I had a gooder bandaid, I'd try fixing you for a million years.

Last stop in their Sunday, they go to the flea market, which, for this small rural town, amounts to an explosion of civic feeling. Not much has happened all day, not much ever will and within the stillness Shanya moves with deliberation before the stalls, eyed by small-towners whose dormant question moves them with a torpid oily sexiness: Could Shanya be Lucy's half sister? That telltale shade and hair—a mixed-race child of a different father? Whose loins linked with the mother of these girls? The flea-market sellers shoot looks between girls and the mother, delimiting borders of tribe and gene.

After great deliberation, from a bored lady with crimped bottle-blonde hair, Shanya chooses a rhinestone-studded black velvet purse—one dollar more than the $2 which Pint's mother had suggested the girls find on cardboard price signs. Pint takes Shanya's lead and chooses a cuddly bear, also for three dollars, because why see limits? Delaying, they are delaying the end of the day, Shanya trying to teach Pint how to balance a plastic water bottle on her head and whenever she starts a game, the mother cheers, feeling the friendship is no well-meaning, benighted enterprise in a landscape where they have sighted so few younger than first-year college students.

Why's it easy for Shanya to balance the bottle? asks Pint, looking up at her friend's hair oil-sheened flat to her head, zigzag-parted into a thick braid at the back, Pint's lower lip heavy, meaning that in two seconds, she could cry and change the afternoon's timbre.

I'm older, my head's bigger, says Shanya. But you're good at balancing balloons!

When they're floppy? Before they're blown up?

We could find a smaller waterbottle for your head, Shanya offers, her charity another staving off of the return to the college, the rite that includes Shanya's nonchalant goodbye inside the car and the careful gleaning of any goods accrued on this outing, all that was painted, found, given. After, during the car drive away, mother and child back to their pair, Pint asks her mother for braids before her slow drift off to nap, head against the safety strap, global lullabies informing her background.

In Pint's mother's childhood, there'd been no safety belts. Hers a town that believed in free speech, busing, and multiculturalism so that early on she'd learned to hate her white face, gone to school with principals named Big Daddy, mastered the Black Panther handshake, been the only paleface in her classes, stayed as silent as she could, avoided as much as she could being beaten up in the halls or on the bus home as much as she avoided the glance of other whitelings, her face like Pint's so obviously ready to cry. One day her friends Danette, Jocasta, and Tiawanna came over and met her fake-friendly grandmother visiting from Saint Louis. The mother thought the point was to keep trying. She believed in Rosa Parks and Claude Brown as testaments of faith, met and memorized Maya Angelou, learned the Robot, early breakdancing, socialized outside her melanin quotient, got the honor of performing in an African dance group. While nothing really changed the basic quotient: irreparable whiteness.

Now because of limited employment horizons, as someone at the top of the food chain put it, they'd moved to a town which enshrined whiteness. Mail-order catalogs which once seemed so foreign presumed this place, a snowy blanket of ignorance, a plaid neverland impossible to imagine in the town she had grown up in, where as she grew in height so did shame about melanin deprivation.

At the flea market, delaying their Sunday goodbye, by the side of the parking lot, the mother starts a game with rocks and sticks: a story about an enchanted forest, one Shanya likes, all of them using high squeaky voices in what is also Pint's favorite game. We're playing puppet! Pint tells her mother.

So lost in puppet they don't notice him at first. A beef hock of a man come over, one of the oversize boys in their fifties you see riding 3K lawnmowers on tracts of land with new seams, farmland quilt being turned inside out to become lawn surrounding cookie-cutter gray colonials with large chandeliered master entrances, sheds, playrooms + dens, two-car garages and avant-garde washing machine–cum-dryer, all with room for a growing family!—the whole of it making Pint's mother hunger for the pretend solidity. Schooled by old sympathies, she suppresses house-lust. She has heard the last of the old family farmers bemoaning the newcomers and loss of the old ways, the farm survivors turning themselves into pick-your-own places and quaint fruit-stands for the new consuming city crowd, purveying nostalgia to keep up income and a shred of family tradition.

Beefhock stands over them, casting a cow-size shadow over their game, and the mother squints up at the aurora behind him. Does she know him? Impossible.

Without preamble, he cuts in, slowly, measuring honey and spite: Who's *this* cute brown girl? directing the question solely at the mother, tongue suggestive, flicked out over his lips before lolling again.

Spines stiffen. *Girl.* Even Pint knows to brace herself, water bottle falling out of her grasp and into the rutted mud next to the man. The crimped-blonde lady seller heaves herself out of her stall, slowly, in a state of permanent regret—loves unreceived, ungiven—to make a big show of handing the bottle back to Pint.

Perhaps the man's voice gives them pause: a man used to making discomfort arrive on cue. The mother's tongue also stiffens but trained in certain scripts manages to say: My *daughter*, placing her hand on Shanya's shoulder. Why? she continues. You know her?

At which the man swishes saliva inside that big cavern of a mouth, choosing not to spit. He backs off, retreating to a private clannish tailgate party with someone who might as well be his twin, against a truck large as a baby dinosaur, spitting again but manacled by pride: he won't try again. The eyes, however, are loud: slut. Easy to imagine his planning of intricate rapes, methodical, bringing lighter fluid, rope. But the moment has passed, they are practically safe; Pint managing to balance the waterbottle for one nanosecond before they get back inside the walls of their car.

Shanya knew more or may be just in the habit of questioning nothing. When she said goodbye, for the first time, goods clutched to her chest with one hand, she actually held Pint's mother's hand, the grasp warm and dropped just as quickly.

While once Shanya leaves, Pint asks, lower lip trembling, rejecting the idea of being replaced: Did her own mother claim Shanya as a daughter?

And if the mother were actually to answer the question, where to begin? Cain and Abel, Ishmael and Hagar, sons of Ham, Anansi stories, Ottoman power, traders, colonial economies, political decisions, cities, infrastructure, American variations on injustice and inequity? Instead with one hand she inserts the lullaby disk, hoping for the soporific of a drive through the farmland's golden divine.

...

The next time they see each other, Shanya gives Pint a book she has written about a girl named Shanya who comes not to be afraid of the magic forest in which Pint and her mommy and daddy live, and all of them together discover the magic treasure and gold coins and become famous because only they discovered it!!! And though people used to be scared of the magic forest, now all people feel grateful to the five of them plus Papa Willie and they all stay famous famous and then magically become presidents of a college for both humans and fairies!

Each weekend Shanya descends to the school with her father, driving more than an hour for him to help the college, servicing entitled students who have lost keys and have urgent needs to heft boxes of technology or keep bikes locked on campus over the summer, kids spilling libido into careless late-night parties, all rim and periphery of the most memorable moments of their lives to be stroked forever in a future papered by alumni requests. They'll belong to this place.

If Shanya's father has a college degree, he's mum. A bit old, possibly Shanya's grandfather, though Shanya calls him Papa or sometimes Papa Willie; gray creeps through his beard. He's seen his share. What he shows Pint's mother is a rough regard, though, as part of his success at the college, friendly enough, he nonetheless gives away zilch. Willie will go so far as to ask how they'd been, or to say he was sorry that Shanya wasn't around. This weekend she's with family, he'd say, a scar traveling down one cheek with its own silencing seam, a credible working man with the stern unquestionable being his love for Shanya and how well she lives in its embrace.

After the flea market day, Pint's mother returns to this: that Willie's granddaughter had sat semi-attended for hours on the stone wall across from the janitorial office, doing nothing. The girl had no book or ball and seemed as if she could use a little diversion. Hours must have been spent as Pint and her mother drove off to pastimes before returning to this sweet-faced girl still watching students file past, earphones hooking them to the mothership, glances flickering significant nihilism.

Those early days, Shanya had been polite, thankful, eager to watch even their small-kid, positive-spin, we-all-get-along videos, sharing in the family's odd Friday night customs, the candles and grape juice.

After Pint's father got promoted, her mother found a more secure job at the college. Summer they left to see family and friends. In August, only the idea of Shanya helped lure Pint back on the plane east, leaving cousins and friends and delicate weather, heading back to August's steam, the rural college and overheated town. Now they need her even more. On the way back to the college, Pint says: Shanya is my best friend.

What does Shanya think about all of it?

Though Willie says his girl missed them over the summer, she betrays little. At the wall, she gets into their car, not under duress, seemingly happy. Lots might be better than being outside the custodian's office hearing student calls about lost keys.

The one story she tells them is about when water waves at an amusement park scared her so much she was like oh my god! Pop culture has started to make inroads. She wears a gold-laminated shirt that says QUEEN and in the car performs precocious little cross-your-heart busty moves learned from cheerleading practice. She tells Pint she's all about cheerleading because another friend Kwaysha, her father's friend's daughter, like a cousin, is doing it too.

The younger girl says: I hate hearing you have other friends, and Shanya laughs.

Practices the moves, one two three! Hands together over her chest, down on her hips, little stabs toward womanhood. Pint doesn't get why cheerleading occupies her so much, or how now Shanya has to stay north certain weekends, forfeit their fun afternoons together, or why it would be fun to cheer someone else's team.

A few weeks back, Pint gives in: Can I cheerlead too? she asks her mother, who hopes only to defer.

On weekends when Shanya doesn't show up on the wall, Pint and her mother proceed from hump to hump, Shanyaless, morning to afternoon, not mentioning any part of their old life back home— the sunny playgrounds, the casualness of playdates, the friends and grandparents—but rather seeking amnesiac pursuits. They perform on the empty stage of the college concert hall, sing about being somewhere over the rainbow on the grand piano, practice hopping down stairs and sometimes run into Pint's mother's gleeful students whose hats are loud as their voices.

One Sunday, Shanya says she couldn't come the weekend before because they had to visit her uncle in prison. One Friday she says she'd stayed overnight with her mother, who until now Shanya never mentioned. When they play hopscotch, Pint's mother asks what reminds Shanya of being Pint's age. The older girl says: If my mother hugs me. Pint's mother doesn't ask more. This Friday, neither girl talks much, sliding into something of a parallel afternoon and early evening dinner. Still the trio has scruples, a vow of allegiance to the secrets behind Willie's face: they always used to make sure, with comic hysteria, to get back on time, by eight because Willie would not want to linger at the college past 7:59, when some imagined steel doors lifted, offering him exit.

That night, sitting down for the meal, a knock comes at the door: the girl's mother, Andrea, lips skinny and scarred, unhappiness clear. She doesn't like to go looking for her girl. Maybe the candles are what startle her as well, maybe they're what make her readier to fight, proof someone might be doing witchcraft on her baby. Her mouth opens and shuts.

By the carillon bells, it is just after seven, not eight o'clock, but Andrea is clearly too mad to speak, managing only *Let's get outta here, baby*, to Shanya who keeps her gaze focused on the carpet until she is gone.

After that, Shanya doesn't come to the college for a long time.

When she does, she doesn't seek them out and Pint's mother also finds ways to avoid the custodian's office. She feels her trespass, holding tight to her office keys, never misplacing them. Easy to elude Willie: his patterns had once been their life-drip. Perhaps the mother once sights Shanya on a path but backs away, cowardice a burn in her throat. Though they all join in this, colluding in the slow fade just as they'd created their afternoons in parallel, the mother rarely mentioning anything that might stir memories, though sometimes she slips: ice cream, flea market, koi.

Can't we see her? Pint asks, less and less often, more absorbed by her nursery school, fall leaves and apple picking, firetrucks, painting, reading. Can't we? One day, won't she, Pint will stop asking. One more bad decision made by the adults, thinks Pint's mother, but could she have handled it better? Had something worthwhile beyond ice cream been exchanged? Or is hope a constant promiscuity? You will be met, you hope, someone will span time with you.

None of them guess that one day Pint will finally make a pilgrimage to find Shanya. All these years Pint keeps Shanya's storybook as one of her most treasured possessions though it is the older girl who breaks the silence first, sending Pint a birthday gift, a t-shirt with her name in bubble writing, sharing her news: Shanya lives not far from the capital's water wave park and is taking college classes between hours at her mall job, a store selling anything airbrushed. The package comes addressed to Pint care of the college where they met, where Pint has just gotten her degree, having become a collector of fallen leaves and nostalgia, a girl who likes dreamy tall music-loving boys with fancy philosophies, a photographer of blurred, impatient figures. When the two girls walk through the depressed capital's streets they might as well have entered one of these photos, Shanya still taller, eyes warm and curious but then hard and flat, back and forth, an odd blurring gaze even as she keeps up a river of small talk between smoking in bursts and telling Pint about customers, all of which makes Pint's throat clench.

The stream of talk makes clear that the day could end and they might have said nothing of substance, leaving them only a fade-out, exclamations and abbreviations, the occasional posting, maybe even a birthday card in bubble writing saluting some idea that either girl needs yearly reminders of their past.

What is not clear is who wanted this day more. Someone did. Both conspired to make it happen. What Pint will wonder is whether it mattered to the older girl the way it had for her, the way she'd kept a private shrine in her heart all these years, Shanya her first love in a new landscape.

The subject that takes over their conversation, apart from the fun to be had in the capital, are the mistakes of parents. Pint's mother dead now some three years after an accident. Her father lives in India, and soon Pint will tap a minor payout and visit him, hoping to figure out the rest of life.

What's your plan? she asks Shanya, who at first looks through her.

That's exactly what counselors at the college say all the time to me. What's your plan?

They get back without detour to mothers, a safer topic, though Pint realizes her big question is whether the whole friendship had been a net hooked up by someone. In her head goes a refrain her mother once used: no asking questions of a dead fish.

My ma's doing better, Shanya says, but Papa Willie passed six years ago.

Sorry, says Pint.

We daughters are left, says Shanya, smiling.

What Pint wants to ask more than anything else is: But do you remember me, I mean *remember* me? Finally she dares it, asking, and Shanya, whose voice can quickly sound like it comes from an older woman comes out burred: Yeah, you were cute.

But what do you remember exactly? Embarrassing to press the point but Pint must, if this will be the last they see of each other.

I gave you rides on my back? I taught you to cartwheel. Oh, and how to use a water pistol. I was the one called you Pint. Sometimes over the years I asked Papa Willie about you. How you were doing. He knew nothing.

Nothing could have been enough. When they said goodbye, some waiting stuck in their hug, full of uncertainty, neither dreaming of starting another sentence.

On the train ride home, one girl will keep asking herself whether even that moment mattered. Did they have anything? A doom lies in having the burdened temperament of a historian. Outside passes the ancient lichen of winter trees, the cold bitten gray of industrial northeastern towns, promising only lights inside apartments and houses. Had the two girls satisfied the renewal of their friendship, all those emails and texts? Or had the memory treasured for so long really just been a little insanity sustained among the three of them, now with only two left?

One weekday, back when she'd been little, Pint had missed Shanya so much she had collapsed in yet another campus parking lot, in her mother's arms but crying out to invoke the warm and convivial: Shanya, Shanya, Shanya! No amount of maternal bribes or promises of eternal fun could appease her. Even years later, Pint will find herself, when stumbling or bumping her knee, saying ShanYA! as if the name could soothe that original place where she had first loved someone outside herself with such great heat.

In that parking lot, she'd sobbed: Shanya! Let's just drive up to her now, she kept asking her mother. Not seeing why the demand couldn't be fulfilled: Let's go right now to her house!

Though her mother's voice had been firm: We can't.

But why not?

It's late. By the time we got there, it'd be time to sleep.

Couldn't we just sleep over? Be there with her?

We can't, her mother had kept saying, a refrain, like a one-way train on a clattering track, a voice with the same whine and chug: We can't!

In Pint had been a hunger to come to the surface, to grasp the answer.

Can't we just go where she is?

We can't. No, we can't—

TALENT

That Chinese take-out menu could have changed my whole life. First I'd had a bleep of trouble stuffing it back in my bag, being it was the last to distribute that day, postal slot here, under a doormat there, up and down pinchy stairs along Half End and its pseudo-cobblestone streets, whole jimey place tighter than your great-aunt's corset, smelling like curry-breathers raised dribbly broods and then left the bunch there to choke on sauce.

This job a shiner like the rest that year, a tickle on the old memory keys but necessary. Only the January before, I could wolf down decent bits of grub and not what became usual for me after my old lady upended me, the standard meal those days paper-wrapped fish-bones that played pinochle in my gut.

If I was half a mind to let the menu blow away, that part ruled with the wind light-fingering the menu so it shot onto the strange sea rocks we kids used to call the dinosaur because its spine lorded it over this corner. All Half End buildings were built to heave around the rocks like someone actually considered the half-pints around here who enjoy clamfooting it after school high onto the plateau for sun-baking even if they get mostly our steady spit-drizzle.

Usually I wouldn't mind but that day my rhythm was off and the thing flew before I saw the kid. Sitting there, not lost or sad, just a big lot of nothing, hunched over, round head and brown bowl hair, cheeks broad, kid humming and picking at something. From below the rocks I called up saying hey, get that? Meaning the menu, because hunger turns my brains into kidneys and otherwise I'd end up lying to Old Skintyflint as to the disposition of the total.

Little Mister Bighead raised his nose to stare. Then smiled, not seeming to understand. The paper? I said, pointing to where the thing had impaled itself.

His smile: that's what must have splinked my coil, since I hadn't seen someone smile that purely in forever. Even the tiniest rat around here has a swindler's grin saying it is ready to suck the inside of your veins clean but this sack was another story. He wanted nothing. Okay, I said, already hiking up, messenger bag pushed back, okay, palms open to show I wanted less. Once I got up he too held his hand out but to show me the treasures he'd been ahum over: three baby snails, shells that soft pukey color meaning in a second you could crush them.

Oh, I said, a person out of practice in knowing how to handle brats. A person like me tends to be better at killing, such as ants one by one or any mite daring to go crazed over my sheets late at night. Never shabby with mice either. But I hadn't seen my own nieces and nephews in maybe twenty years, that's how certain wires had gone all disconnect. The lot of them probably grown now with babies of their own, mewling and hauled off to the dole line. Meanwhile here their uncle scraped by enough to keep a single drafty room with its rodents gone brassy.

You gotta no tongue?

Shouting into that smiling face because otherwise he wouldn't understand and then I saw them, the couple who would not have marked my memory for a second otherwise. Guy with a big walrus moustache and little foreign beard, gut big as if he'd swallowed some walrus preggers and his lady with her pasty face and thick cheesy leggings the kind I'd pass by with no third thought on the train, awkward in her short potato-sack of a skirt, both of them in grays and whites like the sky they were about to disappear against.

When I showed up, they were ahead of the boy on the rocks but my coming clinched the deal. They eyeballed me and then high-tailed it quick over the plateau toward where Half End loses itself and becomes the endless city where I'd spent too long myself before deciding to come home.

Let's say the little lunkhead was seven but even so that foreign-cheeked head of his could have fit on your average fifteen-year-old in my family, we being freckled scrawny runts used to run this whole zone. Never mind—the boy started, blushed, choked. If he couldn't talk, it was spiky clear to me he also didn't want the cheese-potato types to disappear and leave him. Yet he acted as if someone had warned him he had to stay staked to his snail spot.

Maybe I didn't think straight. I was shot, true, had been planning to hit Goa's for coffee after my menu run for hours but I'd pushed past my limit. So the moment was unplanned, which means I'd never creamed anything like it before. When kids used to get trashed in school, or later when we all got stuck inside bigger bodies, same boys now with hides gin-soaked and usually meaner and holding huger grudges, I'd never shown enough spleen to superhero it in to save someone, me the kind to stand by mouthing little bits of nothing like *it will all come out in the wash*. But who can explain what steals a person's usual habits?

His parents or those mousy types had fled and with such guilty looks it was clear this kid had nothing going for him.

So when he didn't speak I tried pulling his hand but he just looked at me like I was some freak landed into his world and when he didn't budge I lifted him sideways like you would a bunch of wet wood. Weird how the boy went limp and didn't fight. Course I did what I could to speed over rocks I knew well. Still, that pair of rascals knew their job. They'd already rounded all available corners and were gone. Way our dinosaur spine works, people can quickslip it into the city's mole tunnels. During our own brat-time, we thought gremlins waited to steal kids to their side of the dinosaur rocks.

Thing to do might have been call the police but then again that could nix anyone's odds. So I stood roiled up inside, *right thing to do, right thing to do*, words meaning I lost any hope at truth, meanwhile trilling out patter to the boy more for my own cheer than his understanding. Sounds funny but those pale eyes stayed unstirred as the bottom of a shell, like the boy could be some sea creature who would understand if I could just tune the blur of sound coming out my lips.

Ten minutes later I'm trying to explain some of this to Goa, my sugar-coffee fixer, boss of the corner kebab place where we had a real boardwalk before the river dried up. I knew Goa from a ways back, not my own kidship but after, when I'd been studley for my lady by doing finish-carpentry jobs in Half End, our place tarpaper because its curvy streets and the way people know what you endure over the course of a day mean you never really dream of leaving.

So Goa stared through my eyeballs like I was last year's fool while my little guy next to me got bigtime into savoring a chipped bowl of rice and egg soup Goa slopped out. For a boy his age, my little guy ate nicely without slurp, least if I remember my own puling nieces and nephews and their spattered bibs.

Come on, no squirtlike behavior, Goa said, call police or they be on you like crabs. He wanted me to stay current with my debts, half his unibrow up like I could've forgotten the prior year's incident, a small thing with someone's car. Natural for me to think Goa's joint was the first place to bring the kid but maybe I'd gone squirrelhead to think he'd show sympathy.

You're saying turn him in to Children's Services? I was asking.

The boy beamed.

Goa was shouting: Fiend, not that, godsakes. They will make you bum official.

What about—? but Goa's look told me there'd be no luck with that, his breed of secrets too thick to dare the light.

So should a person just forget someone somewhere?

But I didn't want to look that neck in the face. Something about the kid's smile. Me as a kid, I'd go with any fellow willing to lop me over a shoulder. Once, a little joiner, I was bouncing in a plastic house filled with air, a big event we all cared for, the house visiting us once a year to lure shoppers into the chain market. The boys always so much bigger than I was and I'd let myself go, head flopping on soft plastic, lying lost, not trying to protect myself as they jumped with neon-colored shoes up and down next to my head, sight awhirligig. My own uncle stood outside because the bouncy-house bouncer wouldn't let him in, shouting at me through mesh: What, boy? You not know how to protect yourself?

Difference being that even if I didn't choose protection, even if I was different in the head, I could always speak. I had already shouted twice in the boy's face You a-deaf? but he just gave me his smile. The people who ran away could have been poor Russians or tired French, given the torn clothes, the guy with that shipbuilder build and his ratty thin girl partner in crime.

All right then, I said, because what, stay in Goa's forever? Goa had errands, never ask what they were, because to stay Goa's friend, I'd found out better not blush or inquire.

So here the boy and I are, walking home, meaning a place to lay a deadbeat body down on nights your coins get lonely in their clink. We're walking past the Museum of Old Things, that eccentric lady with veined sausage legs and old rubber sandals who hides her fortune but keeps changing exhibits in her window. She and I on friendly terms because I did some odd-job plumbing and carpentry back when it was starting up, her whole place stinking of old socks and rotted timber, but she'd taken a shine to me, saying: You're one of those original survivors, just like me. Here we were passing the old-sock museum and this boy could not be persuaded to budge from its picture window. First time he goes balky on me, I'm thumbing my nose but he goes goggle-eyed over the golden piano in the window, kind more for show and not played in two centuries, but he starts tugging at my hand.

What? You want-a to go in? For some reason I think speaking fake Italian will make the kid understand me but jargon or nor, my lunkhead makes his needs known, pulling at me. I have to admit, whole thing cute in the way I used to find my pet ferret until it kept skittering onto the ground where it hunched up and ran away to bilge on my landlord's floors and I had to let it out to predators that still play haunt around our dry riverbed.

So the boy and I go in to the museum. Because it is close to closing, the lady guard who never stops telling you about her hemorrhoids if you give her two-thirds a chance stands there as if shocked seeing me, the old runt, there with some company for once. She holds her tongue and nods, meaning we go in free of charge, my dink knowing he's in on a good deal, staring at both of us like I might also be the one give permission to stroke that ancient piano. She looks around before she nods yes.

But then my jesus, the noise the ballhead squeezes out of the box, able to pull from that cranky eighty-eight something I guarantee no one in a million years heard this side of town or ever, I'm talking St. Martin and Academy and Westminster and who knows what else, no fooling. Not like I haven't been around music, and let me not go on about it but let's say in my head also played some song from childhood about a sprout of his planting and I thought fiddle if this boy is not righteous. Because for once I am not being cheated. Seems the boy is made from some other place, like an angel lying on the mattress I fix up for him at home later, the bed made by stuffing shirts into the too-big suit my uncle left me when he died. Boy humming, staring at the ceiling, and I know I should take him poking around, playing wherever he wants to, not to make coins multiply but because of nature. Screw the cost of lessons or books and whatever bits people might lift.

You're an odd case, I tell him.

He turns and in the half-glow glimmers toward me.

Don't mind the ants, I say, but my voice makes what I meant to say as a question come out more a command.

He gives out a little bark and then stares back like someone declared us in a contest until his eyelids shut the way an alligator's do, a fact I know on authority from my childhood being left for hours at the zoo by my own uncle.

Next day I'm of two minds, due to call at Old Skintyflint's around eleven to see if he wants me to plaster menus over a different zone but by the time the boy and I wake it's almost 10:30 and I want the day to play differently.

My boy's in the same shirt and pants I found him in, I'm muttering to him something about new clothes and we're walking toward the cafeteria where you can pour milk from the coffee area without anyone giving a flying ham. Sugared milk and also a bun from the salad area and you are set far as breakfast. I think: Do I bother schooling him in this? But then we're just in and smooth as you like, he takes the milk and bun like a little gentleman and sits with me outside where no one will bother us and I'm thinking how we look to passersby. Like a father with his bigheaded son, uncle and nephew out carousing, or social worker with his foreign charge out on some special plebe outing?

What happens is we're sitting there and the boy is happy dipping his bun when our usual police siren goes by wailing, the boy quick in covering his ears but in such pain he knocks the milk so it drenches my one good pair of pants. The siren gone as soon as it started but the boy is sorry on my behalf, trying to sop up the stain with his shirt, cringing like he's afraid I'll beat him which rips my tongue out.

Big head or not, the boy whimpers in the tiniest voice.

So I take him to the enormous toy store, not knowing how to handle extras and stalling for time, a place I've always loved. Back of my head thinking isn't it just a matter of time before I hand my boy off to some rich old lady with unstained hands who knows exactly how to handle unwanted charges? Some blameless old biddy who'd use educated tones with the social workers who will then place him in some good family where they have proper bedtime and nutritious mealstuffs and the thought of this so weirdly squeezes saltwater out my eyes, I don't notice at first the boy again seating himself but this time at the little kids' piano against the wall.

I imagine my ex-girl tugging at me and saying Luther, don't be a fool, let the urchin play, leave him right there, but again I'm listening to what this kid pulls out of those keys and me, I've been a sucker for music my whole life, could stand all day listening to a guitar player on the street only starting to tune, what can I say, and this boy's stuff a thousand times better than anything.

People in the store seem to agree, meaning I'm not a fool. Some biddy of the sort I was imagining leaving my little dink with nods approvingly at me: You started him on lessons young? I just nod and take all credit, and though a small crowd has gathered around him, people not even checking phones or watches, just hypnotized by my little snake charmer, wheels are starting to spin and I'm thinking: Well, he could get us out, right?

I mean, it was not really me thinking it, more a certain voice visits me.

After, I pat his back a little too hard, saying you did good and he smiles but less because he understands and more I think because he recognizes I'm a good papa duck and he can lighten up about basic survival.

I take him to Austerlitz Hall, our main performance hall, a non-blight that brings bigger city types to watch shows, but the only one around is the tired old guy with a bookie shade on manning the ticket booth.

Think we might speak with the manager?

Manager? guy says, coming out of a coma.

You know—and here I can't keep up my aping of someone more confident—someone in charge of performers?

Beside me the boy is doing a little one-two step on duck feet, his torso big and almost manlike, I notice for the first time, like some kind of swimmer, but his legs are short. No wonder he has a hard time in life, all that talent squeezed upward.

Concert manager? Half the bookie's teeth smile.

Clearly the pair of us happen to be an odd sort coming around at one in the afternoon on a day there's no concert but the bookie decides to bestir himself enough to put in a call to someone. Yes, okay, alright, he says, glancing down at us, go on up to the second floor.

We push into that rich space and I mean it is rich for someone who has never been. I can taste how upmarket the cigarettes smoked in here would be, resting on my lips, burnt and delicious. Ghosts crowd the space, ladies in perfume and swank men spilling cognac into the rug's curlicues.

On the round marble stairs going up, the boy's small and awkward suddenly. You'll see, I promise him, and he does that little hopeful glimmer like he understands, at least better than that awful whimpering cringe.

To make your time short: the concert manager hears the boy and knows from the first strokes the scoop. The boy's maybe our century's original prodigy, some kind of Russian gone missing on his country's tour. You don't read the papers? Someone trying to get him out of the country. Manager thinks it best to get him to immigration and plot out amnesty. This kind of talent, a kid only seven, could be a search warrant out. You better flee, says the manager. Boy's name is M. N., that's all that's worth knowing, you probably should hightail it out yourself, we'll handle it all.

If I haven't found a lady or anyone else to share life with, I did have a couple of fighting male betta fish in a glass jar for a while until they ate each other, fact the pet store didn't tell me about, you need to keep them separated from their impulses, and then you could say

I probably knew for the last time responsibility's never worth the suffering. Sure there was a time when things could have changed for me but to get back to my boy, did I walk down those stairs with tail between my legs? I did. This old wannabe of me, still in Half End, has some tales to tell. Don't mind my new job, these last years serving as companion for rich old ladies, not out in the world where they need someone in coachmens and cavalry twills but inside where they need someone who doesn't mind them sipping grog while he rubs a foot with lavender talc until they fall into their snores.

But tonight my M. N. is playing Austerlitz. In the posters he stares down his swallowtails, now himself a big broad man. If the wall fell years ago, at least I have not and memory's long. Of course I'm going, unfolding a few bills from between the perfumed scarves of my latest lady and shining my shoes till they look like big blocks of licorice.

Since Goa died of a bad heart years ago, I can't ask him to come. Being as it fell to me to clean up his earthly belongings, I got not only his secret holdings but his suits, though only the one with the most solid color fits.

In the mirror I pull myself straight, imagining being there in a few hours, listening to my lunkhead, now older, playing, and what an airplane that might all be, the music like the life you were meant for shooting off into the sky. I like to think that if he stands and speaks some bad English to the people of Half End, he might halfway include me. This might be the case when, concert over, my eyes drenched, drizzle to full-on storm, I can't stand for the encore and be just one more beast clapping together with everyone in the hall. And then I pull myself together into what matters and get myself out before there's any slightest chance in the world a person could spot me because out is my paradise—out may be horrendous but out is where I know to stay.

THE CHRISTIAN GIRL

That morning, I was not exactly spying on the Christian girl taking her bath outside in the strange area my father had rigged up for her, because though he had managed to persuade the women of the house to let this young girl live with us and eat with the children, this girl who helped us for some vulnerable reason everyone protected which I didn't understand, no one let her bathe where the women did or use the same small chamber pot, since both her bathwater and waste were to be poured out elsewhere and so avoid any mixing with ours. In this way we stayed apart: otherwise her muslin dresses and water-harshed hands were ours, her apples, jokes, and tendrils of hair escaping her bun. Because of this tender reason that had to be sheltered, she had her own place to sleep and bathe. If you stood on the hill just above at the right hour when no neighbor was around, you could see the care she took, placing the animal-fat soap she used, different from ours, on the stone wall my brothers and I dedicated ourselves to dismantling.

She had a way of undoing her hair with a kind of trick so it fell down around that snub face, followed by a bit of shadowy movement through the slats. While watching her, I could not help my own little body-trick starting to perform on its own and could not also help the feeling she knew. Discovery! Or almost and so I panicked, dislodging a piece of rubble toward where she bathed.

To see her through slats was not so different from how she first appeared among us, stepping down the path, wearing a brown dress of a kind we had not seen, something that might have been made from potato sacks and then belted. Never had I seen a person like her, so soft and foreign yet accessible and not hidden away.

Our mother was proper, a person cited often for properness, and though I understood this meant her airs were great and that many failed in their liking, they always spoke of her refinement—all that meant she could read French, Russian, Polish, German, Hebrew, her skirts sheaths long as this education, high-waisted black affairs with tiny complicated buttons up near her waist that fascinated me, the entire sheath of it making it impossible to imagine having come from that concave belly, with only those mysterious buttons offering the hint of a clue. During that time, my mother did not walk so much as sweep through our house, two levels, with an assortment of aunts and others upstairs, but if I watched her swishing too much, a little rush of something flooded my chest, as if I had just punched a pillow and only air puffed out.

My job as the youngest was to warm the beds of each of the women at night before they entered, what they always laughed about: That is what he is good for, little Henryk, I heard them saying, he'll make a good bed warmer, though I never wished to pursue that laugh, one more item adults left in their wake, stealing your attention and then vanishing like a particular small fluff of goose feathers I was sure kept following me everywhere in life and not just when the women beat our pillows on stultified summer afternoons.

My father scared me, a big man respected in the town for his great timber enterprise which in retrospect now seems just a bit of land outside town where he judiciously planted trees and cut them. He called himself captain of the enterprise, an odd, un-Jew-like thing to do for many reasons, I later understood, mainly because Jews did not usually get to own land, but my father was tall, half soldier and half tree, and perhaps this broad-shouldered stance got him favors not granted to others given the pride in his bearing which made him tell anyone he trusted enough that he was descended from a line of rabbis all the way back from the Baal Shem Tov and before that the Maharal of Prague and Rashi and someone they loved to discuss named Dreyfus in the town of Troyes all the way back to a humble sandal-maker in second-century Palestine.

That order I never got straight, I just heard the names so often they whined an incantation. Once my father beckoned me alone to his study, really more a cramped alcove behind the stairs, there to take out a copper box in which the crumpled papers of our genealogy remained, the papers that followed us from town to town, all the sites our grandparents had needed to leave, Lucca and Troyes, Girona and Algiers and Casablanca, with some hint of what the adults called rape either in Africa or among the Cossacks infiltrating the family line before we ended up in our town with its pretty spires and wild forest in which my father's grandfather, blessed be his memory, had seen our future. With him had come the rest of the family and so we settled into a street in the shadow of the church tolling the hour.

Other families arrived as well and from among them my father chose my mother for being the best of the herring, as he said, from among those his own parents had wanted for him, a dark narrow woman with a beak-like nose you can still see casting such shadow in photos, the knowing in her eyes a predictor of prudent values which might spread grace over the large family my father wished to have carry forth his line.

That our mother bore him three boys seemed a good promise at the start. You are so lucky, people said, the family business will work out with sons, and my father's prospects were good, especially since he knew to take unpopular stands in the community such as the moment when someone wanted to dig a well far from the gentiles and my father stood up and said if we are building a well it should be for everyone, not just Jews, in this way doing what he could to shine the reputation of our community, but what did I know, little pisher as the aunts called me, but I overheard everything, how in our town gentiles were more tolerant, leaving one another space, and how especially here Jews bothered to master the foreign language in their homes if not at cheder. True we did keep to our own butcher and baker but apart from that, if you walked the weekday marketplace, you could see everyone, including my mother, sidling through narrow corridors eyeing apples, cabbage, beets with the same scorn, and everyone had the same rough hands roaming through beetle-ridden onions.

My mother had a way of walking like a sentinel through any crowd, an exquisite sight whenever I was lost and looked to find her, her movements bearing a certainty to which you could cling, the angle of her nose such that she never seemed to stop judging. When she smiled it was not as it is with some people, the sun cutting through, but rather more a quick evaluative flash, nothing to rest or bask in for long, hers more a winter sun.

And this may be part of why the Christian girl did something to me as I watched through our one window. She made her way down the small rutted path where my older brothers sometimes hid, their favorite barricade from which they threw stones to chide me for walking up to the road so late in the morning. I was always late, the youngest and dreamy besides, and in their frustration, because I made them late for cheder, they threw pebbles. Not that they were the most eager students once we got to the one-room schoolhouse for boys where we bunched around the table made from my father's timber learning to read the book from every physical angle, like the famous story of Hillel who got cold lying on the snow-covered roof and looking through a hole because he wasn't rich enough to study and hence learned the alphabet upside down, or maybe it was Akiva, this was how my young mind made all stories one, especially those involving threats of discomfort. Not eager students, my brothers, just allies and bullies who loved the act of getting themselves orderly, glossy, and bundled up to get to cheder on time, a place I knew to feel fortunate about since our mother had the habit of reminding us that we had the luck of education only because people liked giving favors to our father, a man who thought himself lucky to employ Jews and gentiles alike, seeing no distinction in who got to be ennobled by manual labor as he liked to say. In his neat shirt, laboriously ironed by one of the women in our house with the heavy steam iron, he nonetheless had the air of a messy scholar, misbuttoned or bearing telltale splotches, sawdusted from where he had kneeled to assist one of his men on the lumber cart bearing logs. So many giant striking trees he had cut down before their prime. As he liked to tell us, the key is choosing the moment just before and then you bring the logs to the larger market in the capital. In everything he did lived instruction, the kind of lesson I should heed, especially that a man could be larger than his surroundings and the stateliness with which you carry yourself makes all the difference.

So that when the Christian girl was making her way down the path, because I was the dreamy one prone to marveling, I saw her first. For a second, with the selfishness the others liked to accuse me of as well as whatever gave me the nickname of Cloud, I watched her rather than go run and tell anyone, which means I lacked any sense of decorum. Mainly because her face had a sweetness I had never seen, a roundness, both her snub nose and mouth twisted to the side under some light in the eyes that asked if you were in on some joke. Only later I learned the light came from a sympathy ready to spring up at all the unfairness of life.

When the Christian girl knocked at the door, I hesitated before opening. Once I did, she did not so much as look me up and down as take me in. Well, she breathed, and in that she avoided the usual formulas of politeness, her exhale describing a world. Which she followed, this sweet-faced girl with her light brown hair and a bad scratch down her cheek, her hands bruised, with something even more astonishing: Well, Henryk?—she knew my name, a flabbergasting fact. I am so glad to see you, she said. Is your mother in?

...

With her strange access to memory or background, I found it even odder that all of the house also knew her, that she would be offered a chair at our fancy table, my mother pouring her a glass cup of cherry tea, and there we had what we'd never seen before, this gentile eating from our best glass plates and cups.

She was something I did not understand at first, a wet nurse both now and in the past, for the two eldest brothers, that strangeness I found acceptable, the two of them always off in their own adventures, but apparently she'd also been this wet-nurse thing for me: I had drunk milk from a girl who looked too young. Plus I could not understand how had she gotten to have milk in her breasts and my mother none?

I stared at her throat and no lower, another mystery, but when she felt my eyes, we both blushed and turned away. Was she actually a great deal older? In my mother's voice I heard a softness she rarely had a chance to show around three boys whom she had to spend so much time scolding.

Given my mother's propensities, I see now, she would have been happier to have had girls whom she might have tutored in French, teaching them to sew buttons or crochet, rather than having to scold three boys forever late for cheder.

That said, it is probable that I was, as my brothers accuse me, her favorite, I the one to whom my mother told a little story when I was sick about three fish swimming through a sea, or to whom she sang lullabies, our home language gargling in the back of her throat like the swish of gills, my bird-fish mother who may have liked me most, since part of my bed-warming duty meant it was always hers I warmed last so that if I fell asleep in my duties, she cradled me in her arms, bony but strong, carrying me gently down to the bed I shared with my brothers. On special nights she let me stay till dawn so that I awoke in tetchy dreams, light muted, finding my mother with her tight bun undone and my feet not affixed to my body until I understood the time had come for me to pad off downstairs.

The Christian girl also had known an enforced time away, that much was clear, and like me she knew how to come back. I tried telling her this once but she didn't understand. I was merely to swallow the new fact of her coexistence with us. We did not have much room but two of the upstairs aunts doubled up so the Christian girl got her own room, rousing some pantry grumbling. Yet we were all to be kind because she had been a help to my mother when she had gone through a difficult time, while the Christian girl had gone through her own hard time, and then all evaporated into a hush, leaving me unclear: Who among us three boys had been difficult enough to cause such hush? Was it the eldest, mostly kind but lacking the decisiveness our mother admired in my father? Was it our middle brother, a great idealist who always fought against my father regarding principles of justice, whether or not we should go to school six days a week or get to ride out with him to his forest? Or was I the one, known for my furtive ways?

My father especially treated the Christian girl kindly. He made clear he did not like hearing my mother give her chores around the house: asking her to lug in kindling, for one, chief among the many tasks my mother hated, much preferring to be upstairs reading one of her books in French or German. Stoking the woodstove meant bringing the mess of my father's business into the house, given the pride he had in his timber's quality and his appreciative inhale when smoke filled the living room. The same fumes made my mother cough. And yet bringing in the wood became the Christian girl's first task. My father cautioned my mother: Give her time, he said, let it go slowly. So much I did not understand, though once I thought I almost understood her snub nose and rounded features by looking into the mirror on a silver brush my mother kept on the dark chest in her room, a softened triangular mirror in which I found the same downward sloped eyes, blue over the same rounding of lips, but then thought as ever I was fooling myself.

...

The day some of whatever balance we had was upset came in the spring, after the holiday we disparaged by calling Kretzmacht which might have actually been Easter. Calling any holiday by such a name was like insulting someone as a pig in the manner of my educated mother, who, when upset about someone barring my father, always exploded in German: Schwein!

Those first months of the girl among us, whenever my mother's voice grew harsh as she could not help flying into a rage at disorder, going around the house whisking after all the female relatives, the ones she called useless, the ones whom my mother's bitter whispers called freeloaders on the hard work of our father and mother both, I liked to imagine I was no child of hers but rather risen from the soft belly of the Christian girl.

We had been told to call her by the familiar name Kir, fitting with the curved mouth and round pink shoulders as well as the cherry tea my mother offered that first day. Once outside near the woodpile I saw the girl fastening hair up in the late afternoon, bright like fire, and horror caught my throat because no way could I leave off staring at her, though I also lacked all excuse if someone caught me in the act. Anyone would tease me mercilessly. This was how we brothers teased, light at first and then narrowed inevitably toward my clumsiness, a long trail of broken china and glass cups behind me, and despite it, sometimes alone among the boys I was pressed into service, going to the market with both my mother and the Christian girl though, increasingly, my mother failed to go, and there we would be, the Christian girl and I in the market, fingering items, between us sharing an understanding with no wheedling needed, a pair like all the others around us, two men with arms swinging in gentle rhythm together, arguing with the same concert of gesticulation, two trees leaning toward each other, the rattle of horses bearing their sawdust scent, and for me the Christian girl stayed a spot of grace and bringer of good things beyond just the tart apples she slipped from a tree only she knew about. She had a way of taking me in. No one else bothered trying since I was youngest and lesser in everything, at cheder especially, only like my mother in that I was good with languages, the one asking questions but always failing to do the kind of brilliant thing our middle brother did, what came easily to him, able to put together two concepts the teacher had introduced. Our eldest brother liked school less than machines, liking to watch a special blade our father had in his factory go round: When I'm older, he said, I'm going to have a factory that makes machines like this, but we laughed since he was clearly going to be a rabbi, the job our family cut out for eldest sons, as my mother had explained, a line going back epochs, only interrupted by the giant lowering force in the sky that sometimes pointed our way and which I could sometimes see, a needle like a cloud compass slanted over the spires toward our home. Then too my throat would tighten. Mostly the adults spared children the stories but their attempts were feeble: you always ended up knowing more than you wanted about this one being killed or that one being burnt out of his house, a knowledge round the rim of things. Others also saw the needle, even those who moved in among us who had heard that in our town of spires the gentiles let you be despite the firebrands elsewhere. What they told us of elsewhere we pocketed, information kept among other keepsakes, though my father kept having difficulty with one man, not just jealous but with some power in town since he was friends with the alderman intent on cutting up one section of forest, but our father's work lived in a world apart from our sellers and our baker, a woman with a great heart-shaped face and a warm salute for any one of our family, helping place us securely. No one had to fear, the needle slanted elsewhere, we were made of rituals as ungiving as my father's lunchtime borscht.

On most days my father returned home to eat borscht the Christian girl prepared the way he liked, an island of cream floating in its center, at its crown a sprig of dill from the small patch I got to tend alongside our house. Before the Christian girl came, the borscht was the rare technique my parents had to show whatever affinity might have brought them together, whatever craze induced them to stand like stiff-necked marionettes in their wedding daguerreotype, grand and unreachable. Until the advent of the Christian girl, the ritual stayed part of the mystery that went with my mother's buttons, but afterward, my mother retreated from her lunchtime service, no longer sitting with him to discuss the house and children, the timber or the nearby tenant farmers who resented my father's holdings. Instead my mother stayed upstairs reading in the room she had to herself, while the Christian girl served him borscht and then retreated.

On such a day and moment, I watched the girl, knowing both father and mother occupied themselves with staying apart, while for me the girl was the axis and entirety of what mattered in the paschal light of an unseasonably warm spring, everyone said as much, how early the warmth had come, until a disruption came from our front yard, someone pushing open the sturdy gate made with the best timber, coming in to whack the ground with a strange tool, mallet on one end, axe on the other.

So surprised, I slipped fully on the hill and came down, landing on my rear not far from where the Christian girl bathed, her eyes peeking at me above the slats. Henryk! she let out. From the front of the house came commotion and yelling, the girl pulled a cloth around her bare shoulders and from different corners we entered the front yard to face the intruder, a young man swearing in a Polish so foul and thick I understood only a few words before he did the strangest thing, lunging forward to grab our girl.

From the house, from his solitary borscht, my father emerged and with a speed that astonished me took in what was happening and moreover knew what to do: he lit immediately upon the boy wielding his axe-mallet so that he dropped the Christian girl's wrist. My father's usually watery eyes were pure steel, asking in clipped Polish what the boy meant by this display and with his head indicated the girl should retreat, he would handle the situation. What followed was a long series of rebukes of which I could only make out part, pretending to fix my eyes on the mottled birch, my favorite tree in our front yard on which I had spent many hours climbing to read a book, the act uniting the faraway worlds of my parents.

The young man kept on and yet my father managed to back him out of the gate which he then bolted. From the front door the Christian girl, still only half-covered, called to us.

Don't worry over such foolishness, my father said before shockingly coming to her and, with the back of his hand, the slightest of gestures, caressing the round cheek with more closeness I had ever seen him show my mother. It will be fine, don't worry. From the upstairs window where apparently my mother had watched everything as well came her voice, a high whistle caught in it: You see what I said?

This was not the last of the troubles coming from the Christian girl. It was already the full blast of summer, we boys no longer needing long pants, behind us that terrible spring sabbath when untimely snowfall induced us to avoid temple to instead sled down a hill on a piece of wood one of our father's friends had given us, only to mistakenly skid past the window in which my father prayed with other men, foreheads and upper arms binding them to a place it seemed impossible for us to reach, where we should have been, what was meant as destiny. Our father knew everything. Especially that we were capable of great sin: on the sled I sat in the middle, the eldest behind, the middle in front, and our father looked up and caught of all eyes only mine, his belt later the hardest on my backside.

All that history happily lost to snowmelt. In the summer everyone grew kinder, even my mother who nonetheless, ever since the incident with the boy and the Christian girl's shoulders, became colder around the house, her entries into rooms less swish and more glacial whiff, something that made you feel how bitterly impossible was the compensation for some initial cost. She had a good head for figures, my mother, another trait which those around her, the aunts living off her, praised, and yet this talent for figures meant she often could not help speaking the language of accounts. I'd hear her tell my father with his watery gentleness that he had incurred an unre-payable debt given his stepping forth to protect the Christian girl, bare-shouldered. My brothers took in none of this. Only I was cursed with memory, as if I'd be forever alone in watching the dancing news of gazes.

The second time, the boy came to our gate wielding no mallet, his hair oiled into a strange part and with his peasant parents, the mother in a belted dress and worn shoes, face identical to those dried apple dolls I saw at the outskirts of market, sold by a man in a red cap whose arms were strangely short, just as the boy's father's arms were, making them all of a piece as I sat there openly gaping from our birch.

This apple doll family came to yell and gesticulate and make meaningful glances toward their boy who this time stood silent, hands opening and closing as if he were pumping air into himself, as if he tried to stay afloat in the presence of parents who kept on with their weathered hands punching the air and then, most surprisingly, they pointed at where I sat stilled in the crook, where I ate an apple while pretending to read one of the picture books my mother loaned me from her childhood. And then the question seemed to involve something with my pulling down my short trousers. But most horri-bly, this marked the one time in my life my father apologized: some-thing grave could be happening. He took me with the other man to the back where brooms, mops, and axes were kept, and there I did not understand what was expected.

Pull them down—my father said, the soul of gentleness after a minute in which it was clear that I didn't know.

And there they looked, the man reaching out with great crudity I still cannot fathom, taking my small bit to turn and examine it until to my horror it did its little trick. In the corner of our yard, a dog which had followed the family choked down what might have been the remains of a dead bird, looking around guiltily as if someone would come for it. I was nowhere I could imagine as the man did his work, unable to reach my father's gaze, given his stature, so instead watched the dog gulping down its food. The argument seemed to do with whether or not I had been nursed by the Christian girl and somehow this matter could be resolved by looking in my trousers. So went the way of the adult world, nothing I could master, not like the grammatical word families we tried mastering at cheder.

Apparently whatever I had done or not satisfied the unhappy family or satisfied them enough that all of them went on their way, my father pressing some meaningful coins wrapped in a handkerchief into their hands, the timber of the door creaking shut behind them. Afterward, my mother and father exchanged a look which I could not understand.

You need to get that gate fixed, she said.

But when the firebrand people wanted to come in the real Christmas of that year for my family, when all of us would need to leave, the people who first gave us the message were those of this same apple doll family, and so we made our way out, only the Christian girl on the hill with her goodbye an unchanging glance as we left before dusk, in my mother's market sack only the copper box with the story of all of us. We could take nothing but what we were wearing, seven layers of clothes on each, so that even my tall mother became as round as the Christian girl. And because my father believed the apple dolls, we survived, and because they didn't, all the rest of my family, our stubborn aunts and cousins and friends, those who lived with us and those who did not, those who worked for my father or nearby, all of them stayed so that they might be killed and because of this I gained strange faith in the power of all that my trousers dropped had been able to do for our family in getting us spared to leave and does it really matter for how long I remained such a dreamer?

CODA

QUESTIONS OF TRAVEL

Is it better to have stayed here and thought of there, Elizabeth Bishop asks, in her 1956 poem. Take Barcelona, ever so pleasing Barcelona. Or don't take it, not quite yet. I am still holding onto Barcelona as a possibility, because to let go of Barcelona would mean a kind of death.

On my first visit, just out of high school on a bohemian budget ramble through France with a mostly best friend, an unlimited railpass trip during which we slept under rowboats and had mussels at fishermen's bungalows, the city was just a train station to pass through in the soundtrack of the new pulsing self, so blind were we, seated on the ground at the Barcelona train station, picking at a stale baguette, so wrapped up in the adventure of being together, seventeen-year-olds abroad, counting coins while talking to random Scots who might as well have worn feathered hunting costumes. Using fantasies about the moment so musical they blocked most reality and even our fantasy of the one to come, we believed we had deciphered the world. My francophone friend made only a small allowance for Spain, because she liked the diffident heroine of *The Sun Also Rises*, so we skirted into Pamplona the day the bulls ran and then fled.

A few years later, having received a grant leading me to Yeats in Sligo, hoping for some red before the green of that summer, I headed first to two cities in Spain: Granada and then Barcelona, and so my real entry to Barcelona involved holding a guitar a Granada gypsy's family had sold me (another story).

Who knows what youth is really looking for? I clung to that particular determination which whispers, constantly, that adventure has an ultimate meaning, that travel works as an end and good in itself. Does later-life travel declare or undo the self in a similar way? Young travel certainly makes you feel the potential energy of who you might become, granting the gift of your wings unfolding to a fuller span so that you return to familiar ground a high flier, never the same.

Travel at most ages and you can find physical constraints paradoxically freeing: the lack of obligation lets you better recognize the cramping of your own mind. The peril and joy of no attachment, no one knowing where you are in a certain moment, can inspire awe, Freud's vision of the all-swallowing libidinous oceanic. Early that return trip to Barcelona, I swam the sea in Cadaqués, overseen by Dalí's crazy house, and had something of an epiphany a quarter mile out, knowing I could drown and no one who cared for me would have a clue where to look, a strangely peaceful realization. The sea's eros and thanatos made all strivings needless: no matter the form I took, deliquescing algae matter or college student, I would be part of the bowlscape of sea and land, a crazed museum poking the empty sky.

Travel, and you are looking out a train window at landscape you will never walk through. You wave at a beaming beautiful child with whom you will never talk. All these thanatos edges—the limitations, the temporality—tighten with the anticipatory eros of novelty, as well as, if you are on a budget, the pleasant and slightly OCD stricture of making do in a city you don't know well.

Back in Barcelona, because of the budgeting, I found myself having coffee in a true dive on La Rambla, a long esplanade of mercantilist desire off which you could find the tiny winding Roman-era street of the hostel in which I was staying, a place with a pleasant, mute block-bodied proprietor never to be sighted without his broom. For whatever lucky reason, I'd been happy to score a single room in his hostel, and the proprietor and I understood each other. Though Franco had died long before, a leftover spirit of protest hovered over Barcelona, an enjoyment of freedom: surprise luxuries and messages combined like cheap strong incense everywhere in the air, in the signs proudly in Catalan as well as, back then, their translation in Spanish. If cultures have an age, the age of Barcelona was also in its early twenties. Faces turned up toward the sun like lily pads in the café at the bottom of the Plaça Catalunya from which the Rambla spilled, and people from all classes issued Catalan consonants with glee, abandoning the Spanish lisp, feeling the happy sting of brazenness.

To be in Barcelona then meant something not wholly unlike what it might have meant to be in East Germany a decade-plus after the wall came down, awake after a long hibernation, the seedy underground and murky edges happy to stretch out. Hence in Barcelona among the gilded street performers imitating the monuments of pre- and post-Franco, awaiting coins from the very few tourists, were the prostitutes of all genders and outfits, the transvestites much less perfect than they are today. Back then, was it not the case, everything was less professionalized than in our celebrity-waistline moment: private fancy triumphed over will and all overflowing with a collective, sloppy-belted charm.

And everything of the city showed the palimpsest of decades of bad thinking from the Franco administration, like the historic modernist building covered over with a bad façade, a garish glass-fronted neon shop selling luxury leather handbags.

A few days earlier, in a burst of optimism, I had actually gone looking for a writing job—I had the lark of a thought that I could support myself as a writer though I'd begun college as a biology major and had ended up a painter, my easel alongside people who would go on to become art-world stars. Yet an almost Marxist objection to the amassing of objects painting requires had grown in my parochial mind: did I really wish to produce coffee-table topics and commodities for the elite via the New York gallery system? The stink of capitalism and vocationalism filled our studios: my fellow students had started narrowing their inquiry into series easily understandable by gallery directors. Naïve, I thought writing was more democratic, and surely I might find a job with my writing, and while I had worked as an assistant (for a puer former psychologist turned fashion photographer), in retail (a dance-clothes store), food service (college dining halls, alumni reunions, folk-music cafés), should I not be putting a little capitalist pedal to the dreamy artist metal? Or mettle, as it were, and did I have enough to make a go of it, everyone in my family a scientist and how would I support myself? No matter how you looked at it, somehow one had to link art and market, support oneself with the thing one loved: Or was that not the path?

Therefore, in Barcelona, I ended up answering a newspaper job ad for publicidad, thinking it meant publicity-writing, and only because they needed someone with the look of an extranjero, a person from beyond the pale, the older manager sent me to have photos done, some kind of publicidad modeling, a task I accepted because why look gift horses in the mouth however mealy-mouthed the specious beasts?

Especially since the grant failed to pay for all aspects of travel. And, after a stint in Granada among the Roma who live in white-plastered caves across from the Alhambra, my wallet had started to thin out in inverse proportion to my curiosity.

There is a book I love reading with my children, one of those William Steig books in which a happy little pig named Pearl goes out to enjoy herself and quickly finds a magic bone which can talk and do magic, ending up by saving both of them from a very suave fox, and I think this magic bone sums up a lot of the way I used to travel and still feel about it, the art of travel as well as the art within it. The magic bone I always had back then, in this case, the thing that justified everything, the thing that sucked everything into its needy little core but could sometimes save me, was the part that thought it saw the world through the optic of art or art-making or being on the side of the outcast flaneur.

Many arts offered themselves: I was doing that most American thing and especially Californian thing of showing varying degrees of focus and exposure, trying to understand whatever small carrots had been thrown my way and whether or not those linked with what I felt drawn to do: reading, taking notes, dancing, playing music, watching people and film, drawing and painting, the idea if not the practice of sculpture. Some Rabelaisian discord of appetites moved me, and what could speak to all these interests? Would only film be the most generous medium, allowing the totalizing artwork of aspiration?

Back in the homeland I might go out with a backpack in which, were you to examine its contents, you could find, on any given day, a sketchbook, a 4B pencil and gummy eraser, a little notebook for ideas, a book, a leotard. Did I lack focus or was I burdened by hunger? Because it was the arts I wanted, the arts in any form, which traveled along with a certain freedom of movement and the body, the body along the edges of the main institutions. The artist walking cloaked like a mod in sixties London or Baudelaire in his cape breathing in the bourgeois or syphilitic streets of Paris, always a kind of clairvoyant flaneur at the edges of a city like Barcelona.

And why is it that some people as they develop move the eros of new sap flooding their veins less toward the idea of all the potential mates around them, treating them merely as happy corollaries, and instead let art be the sun for all tropism? Why do some subvert evolution with the desire to make art? Even animals do it, make gratuitous artistic creations: consider the unnecessary nests of the weaverbird or birdsong itself, as Rothenberg does in his book *Why Birds Sing*.

How does the world of imagination become so filled with light, like Bergman's magic lantern in *Fanny and Alexander*? And why through that optic of artists or art-making does the world open itself with such promise, offering explanations of alienation, fulfillment, color, wonder, even sex? All the books, movies, and sculptures to be known and recognized like distant family members lining up to be embraced and brought into your fold, so much better than any living person to understand all you want to say with your inchoate young self. Link with art and any leaf hanging on a tree promises a story, its own understanding of form and metaphor, obelisks, spirals or death, all of it boiled down to one thing: the need to look and seize the moment. This seemed the gift. With art came the moment. Train enough in seeing and feeling, think of all your artistic predecessors as patient uncles and aunts, and then you too would learn to recognize the aura around the banal, as when Benjamin unpacks his library. Passages you may have noted, paintings before which you have stood, films you have swallowed whole: all of it could begin to direct your attention so long as you stayed open.

And how well, with its modernist architecture and open-spirited port spirit, can a city like Barcelona capture all that is youthful, all that hungers for meaning in a life of looking at things and taking them in.

A premise

In every culture or concern, find a rise and fall away from the simple toward the baroque. The Kuikuro tribe of Brazil living in the high Mato Grosso uses prehistoric methods of hunting and foraging, yet finds it beautiful to implant in the chins of its young children, by very elaborate process, a long, chiseled bone from a monkey spine, and so indigenous kids lounge deep in the Mato Grosso jungle on a hammock from prehistoric time with bones jutting out of their chins like the calcified hipster beards dipping toward caffeine iterations near any Seattle tech start-up. Ballet in the seventeenth century evolves toward an increased complication before hand movements become starker, serving narrative, before moving again toward the nuance of filigree and elaboration. Japan's early Edo period invited in detail and thick walls before returning again to the primacy of light and balance. In the West, the High Renaissance becomes Mannerism, Impressionism becomes Modernism becomes Pop Art, and the way the physical carries the spirit gets essentialized before it undergoes mitosis, never as radical as it thinks it is, because the pendulum between filling the page with detail and essentializing it has its back-and-forth arc, the revolution staying consistent.

So in life. Move toward the specific, the painfully deliciously specific, and you start to find that this particular person matters, that place forms you—cf. every romantic love song written by a singer midtwenties—and then as you age you branch toward the undifferentiated sky, soaring a bit in the broad sweeping patterns. Not just that a friend always behaves a certain way in a certain situation, too disappearing or present, too much the prey of some new line of thought, whether AA or Buddhism or a charismatic therapist wielding any totalizing world view. Get older and you know certain holidays as necessary or needless. You know your traits, say, that you see the world more poignantly after a film, more sharply after an exhibit, a certain kind of dinner party or discussion. Enter a new milieu and with x-ray vision you quickly sight patterns of community and withholding, friend-making and caution. Older, you meet a new person, whether five or eighty-five, and see how every person contains a little world of autism and radical acceptance. Life becomes something about being on a train in which every place has its own borders and stern guards and boundary crossings. A humorous strangeness, a defamiliarization, appears in how understandable or recognizable people start to seem, how open- or close-minded, despite whatever particularity to which they or their tribe cling, their particular form of monkey-spine extruded from their chins.

Older and broader patterns obtain, large Rothko-like swaths of colors with nuance present as you gaze at the color field. The nuance is the eros offered up by your mature sight, a little lagniappe for you to savor even as you note the tango of the back and forth. Older, you note these broader patterns but paradoxically you start to move again toward the specific. Is this the most moribund form of eros? Or one of death's most erotic forms? Each little edge of everything matters. My dying father truly appreciated the owl of the east and owl of the west that started their hoots each day alongside his house in the dark before dawn. Having worked too hard his midlength life, having made workaholism his habit and teleology his addiction, being an adherent to a certain eschatology of ease and abundance—one day there will be enough for the family, one day I can do less—he finally slowed down enough to attend owl hoots instead of waking to begin the day's titrated caffeine and any given day's self-flogging toward a consistent goal.

Children care about the little. The meniscus of water making a small air-bubble below a faucet, careful tracks in snow following a friend's gargantuan strides, a bakery's buttery waft, a tree angled perfectly for climbing, the gaze of an adult. And yet the old also care about the little: consider how retirees take up highly specific acts, a particular pool class, the rhythm of swing dancing, perfecting the swing in golf, gardening in raised beds, which club they join, which card they play in the dwindling game, the owl hoot.

To be specific is to be young again, to care about the phenomenal world. To be broad, to let things go, is adult, but also speaks to some unchanging inner witness which we sometimes can access. When you start to choose the specific, you know where you are on the spectrum toward the recognition of whatever wisdom will wash our mind clean in the last moment before death. Whatever its mineral composition, the dirt over us, the cloth or flames, all will be the same.

What, among other aspects, is so hard for the new parent is the deep-sea change between being someone on one spectrum, moving toward abstraction and pattern recognition, and suddenly becoming one who must be so unerringly specific: reaching for the exact crook of the arm for a nap to take place. Inflate the balloon the right size, so big! Invite the happiness-promoting kids to the birthday party. Become a parent in our era in which parents are asked to be all ages and you become someone who can will a particular slowing down (death, abstraction) into the specific (life). Whether or not you have kids, people who thrive in later life have learned to master the ease of switching gears between the broad pattern and the most specific note.

Second premise

So if maturity offers perspective on foreground and background, routine can sometimes become a transvestite substitute. Routine can make it seem as though all wise choices have been made. Now you might just as well settle in for a long winter nap, habit your blanket, predictability your pillow, the illusion of a life without fears your dream.

If this is the case, art is terminal adolescence, meant to wake you up.

The detail, the angle of sight in *Las Meninas*, in which Velázquez's mirror puts you into the painting itself—all stays urgent. Why did Picasso spend some four months creating sixty obsessive studies from *Las Meninas*? His life as a man may be less than exemplary but his artistry in understanding playfulness, self-authorization, the intensity of the gaze and rigor stays one to emulate. Getting perception right means you have stayed awake. Perceiving your moment right now: the snow skewed in its falling, the messy field of hair atop a child saying goodbye, the last letter you got before she died. Awake, young, old, everything can seem important and connected, not necessarily part of a larger design but arbitrary, asking you to care nonetheless, to pinch yourself awake with the detail.

Barcelona, continued

Perhaps the day after the modeling photos, a collection to which I would never return, leaving them deposited in the coffers of a place called Imatge somewhere in the bowels of Catalunya, I was still thinking my coffers were at an end: and so, the dive, the coffee. In the dive, and what was I doing, taking small beatnik notes in one of the many tiny notebooks I've had and lost, so many over the years—the art of losing isn't hard to master, as Elizabeth Bishop says elsewhere—an actual duck came waddling toward me, coming to wake me up.

Between table and chairs, a duck!

In one of the casuistic or adventitious moments of travel, a strange opportunity waddled toward me. A plot turn: a live duck as if fleeing its fate from the kitchen or basket of a gypsy. In those days, in Barcelona, you could still see far more Roma when now you only see them on the buses or at certain intersections, good as New Yorkers in their wish to wash the windshield of a fuming, spitting, idling car.

The duck must have made me laugh in surprise because I caught the eye of two boys eating nearby, both French, but one, Pierre Sanchez, of Spanish extraction. His friend was blond and uncertain, all energy connected at his Adam's apple, suffering from airy detachment from life, while Pierre was of the streets, had played in Annecy with the great jazz festival, as easy as a dusty sandal, and right off showed that grace and relaxation you find in those who have survived war zones, bad education, absent family, ambition ill fit to birthright.

How did we end up talking just enough? How does a casual conversation over a duck lead to a night in which only Pierre and I went to see jazz in a crowded bar he favored? There Pierre sat in on a set, a skilled trompettiste, fluid and capable of bringing the swell of emotion the trumpet knows almost as well as the French horn, the deep brightness of things unsaid and growing. Small and wiry, he flashed ease and grace and already I was entering some story with him.

I can live on a baguette a day, he bragged. That night he ventured the idea that I should busk with him in the square outside La Catedral, the huge main square outside one of Gaudí's earlier masterpieces. I was, it should be said, no one's idea of a guitarist, being closer to a pianist prone to improvisation. The semester before at school, in response to the end of a relationship, I'd started a girls' band at school in which all four guitarists played just a few crucial chords. Our band's name was Watershed and our big moment came in playing some festival at our school, for which we had a poster, using an image linked to Borges about The Enigma of Choice. Some boys famously thought that poster showed a rain of vaginas, but I cannot ask the lead guitarist about her pick of it, an Iowa writer now dead a few years. That none of us played brilliant guitar deterred us not a jot: not only were we a garage band, we felt we had imbibed something by proxy, to various degrees linked to boys with calls upon the idea of playing rock, some of whom went on to heights of fame, some of whom abandoned such youthful concept soon as the suits came knocking, rock being defined as a juvenile way station. My own ex-beau had lamented to me, with sincere angst, I can't imagine playing rock after twenty (though still drumming). It was enough for me to have learned whatever noodling I had, and to have thought I could learn gypsy guitar, which I had actually learned in Granada, a little, from a family of gypsies with whom I lived in a cave.

And so in Barcelona with my guitar, the next morning I took Pierre up on his invitation and found him in the shade by the stairs leading up to a non-Gaudí cathedral in the Barri Gòtic, the gothic neighborhood. Of contemporary songs, I had Neil Young's simple "Heart of Gold" down pat—*I crossed the oceans for a heart of gold*—which I taught Pierre, and also "Cinnamon Girl" with its strange string-tuning. He knew enough to teach me "Whiskey."

We were an odd pair, a pair of convenience or congruence, playing outside La Catedral. Even when I was just tuning up, clearly no one's adept, people would toss coins into my open blue plush guitar case. Either those passersby felt pity or recalled their own youthful foolish hijinks and selves: their coins' arcs seemed markers of such recognition. Sometimes when a coin dropped, the passersby appeared to know something I didn't about how this moment might look to me later: enviable or lost, the beginning or end of something, none or all of that, but surely awake.

Or else they were just in the habit of throwing—coins, stones, who cared? Hear music and you throw, much as my daughters, in Barcelona on this last trip of mine, always wished to coin-toss toward the most random supplicant, the beggar, the cartoonist, the human making himself into a monument about stasis.

...

Return

> We're only here for a short while. And I think it's such a lucky
> accident, having been born, that we're almost obliged to pay
> attention. In some ways, this is getting far afield. I mean, we
> are—as far as we know—the only part of the universe that's
> self-conscious. We could even be the universe's form of con-
> sciousness. We might have come along so that the universe
> could look at itself. I don't know that, but we're made of the
> same stuff that stars are made of, or that floats around in space.
> But we're combined in such a way that we can describe what it's
> like to be alive, to be witnesses. Most of our experience is that
> of being a witness. We see and hear and smell other things. I
> think being alive is responding.
> —Mark Strand

This winter we came back to Barcelona and I say we because those
coin-throwing daughters and my husband came, all supported by a
different if equally genial grant which, in this case, required me to
see as much of the contemporary art and literary scene as possible so
as to better understand how sectarian tensions were reflected in the
cultural production of the city, or some agglomeration of all those
highly academic nouns. To put it most directly, if I could expand my
international vista, my teaching would improve. If I could just get a
wider, if more specific, view of life right now in a corner of the world
rapidly molting, I would be better. That was the grant's idea, a giant
suckling head offered up on a gilded plate, apple in its mouth, ready
for consumption. I cannot make fun of it, or I can: I proposed it and
we ate the apple.

We came, together as a family, the idea being that we would be
together and I would work in the stolen hours and then they would
leave and I would work even more in earnest. That was the idea.

The vision that had first inspired writing the grant had included
this: I had come across a postcard of Parc Güell, Gaudí's playful park,

one which you may have visited, or perhaps you've seen its image: a series of mosaic-covered benches twinkling in the sun, broadcasting all the playfulness of the mosaic self you too might know in such a place. I had the thought of bringing both daughters but especially the youngest, prone to architectural construction, to such a place: Gaudí's conflation of imagery, his ability to bring together paradoxes, the biomorphic with the gaudy structural—forgive the pun, but it occurs also in Spanish, in a different form—it could inspire revolutions.

As an organism, my family sometimes feels as if it is a mobile artists' colony, those moments when I realize that each of us works on projects near one another: my mate sketching, the youngest involved in elaborate tiny doll dramas, the eldest reading or sewing, the way I might be pecking at a book. Some mates and families do best with projects and the world of responsibility, say, building a table together, organizing camping gear; while we seem to thrive away from more extrinsic responsibilities in some kind of dreamy flow, and so we looked for ways to make my research part of the moment being together. I was to see Gaudí to know how current artists departed from him, the Gaudí I'd never seen much of in that bohemian busking past, and the wealth of this created a broad enough mission. At noon one day, we bought tickets for the next day to the Sagrada Familia, Gaudí's unwieldy masterpiece, the vast unfinished cathedral which these days, in overcrowded, post-Olympics Barcelona, inspires lines of WWII-spared descendants snaking around the corner, a mix of Spaniards, Japanese, German, and French busloads descending with cameras to document that they too have been here and then here, hordes about whom locals complain, though not wishing to look their own gift horse in the mouth: visitors photograph Barcelona's quaintness constantly, at this site, and then in this other site, too, half-attending to specificity while ignoring how much any particular in a photo album is a subset of the generic. And anyway why is it that we need to feel that our trajectory and vision is singular? Why must we feel our march across the earth is unique?

That day, the Sagrada Familia ticket-buying was a way station: we were heading toward the goal of the trip, in other words, the picture on the postcard, the Parc Güell that had inspired the grant that had inspired our long flight, a strange circuitous spice-route flight through Istanbul toward Barcelona.

On the subway to the park, my older daughter noted how many Barcelonas coincided: the cleaner Barcelona, the part of Gràcia in which we were staying, made up of planned hexagonal grids and luxe stores, as well as the Barcelona of the subways, a dirtier zone. A perfect transvestite flashed advertisement-white smiles at the kids, but the train was too crowded for anyone to note this.

At the Lesseps train station, we might have bought tickets for our more immediate entry to the park but, drawn to escape the subway, the kids sashayed forward and we ran to catch up. We followed the line of people moving inexorably like a sullen river out of Conrad along the sidewalks of the upper Gràcia neighborhood and up the huge hill toward Parc Güell. The faces reminded me of a little-known Kinnell poem about joggers which I recall, correctly or not, as having this line: Their faces tell there is a hell and they will reach it.

It seemed wise that someone head more quickly uphill to get our tickets, so I told my family we would meet at the top, where, to my surprise, I found a line to end all lines, a formidable line made up of sublines, conduits, diverters, line administrators, soothsayers, graphs, maps, timetables, and ropes, the line itself a kind of destination. Of course, this was Christmas week, and on another week the sublines and conduits might not have existed; perhaps we might have been able to enter. But we were there then, this was our day to see this postcard-documented place, and though the line's grandeur took my breath, I was ready to stand, a willing soldier in the trenches of tourism.

In its way, the line was not unlike the art piece I would see later in the week, alone, at the Arts Santa Mònica exhibit at the base of Las Rambla: a pillar covered with tiny mirrors which you, like a package tourist, could place in picturesque spots, at the top of a mountain, say. An old-fashioned selfie pillar: you would see yourself reflected against the landscape from many angles.

So in that monumental line I stood while my kids and mate kept hoofing it up the hill, still some half hour away. We had one phone between us. I borrowed someone's to tell the family how to find me in the line. Some lines ask you to enter what we as a family had seen while living in Cuba, the Communist line which asks of its adherents a kind of existential putting-on-hold. You forget yourself and must put yourself on hold.

But this line was of a very different order, seeking to keep you alert, with up-to-the-minute dispatches. Important representatives of the government holdings were dispatched in their blue smocks to answer questions about the line. Only so many people could walk the hallowed grounds at a time.

It is probably fair to say that all of us in line, if in different terms, had come to what we had thought would be sublime in order to dislodge ourselves. My memory, from having invited my sister to this same park years earlier, was that there had been no admission fee, no line, and that only a few desultory types wandered the terraces of Parc Güell. But surely my memory lacked the permanence of a monument or even the structure of this line. Every few minutes one of the blue-smocked people would come around to our crook in the line to flip a sign. Had we gotten our tickets at the subway station, we would've been able to enter at 3:30. But now it was 4:00, and then 4:15, 4:30, 4:45, 5:00—the time anyone waiting in line could enter. In winter, darkness would fall at 6:00 if not 5:30. Grumbles rippled backward. All this wait and for only an hour, a half hour, of witnessing.

As Elizabeth Bishop asks: Should we have stayed home and thought of here?

My mate and kids would still not make it up the hill for the next twenty minutes. Though I was bookless, a romantic tragedy started unfolding right in front of me. There stood the kind of French woman who in her youth had been, perhaps, a seeker of sun and men, a bouncy scamp on Greek islands or the budget Costa Brava holiday. It could seem odd that her neck and back alone told me this but I would have bet my cherished place in line on the certainty. She lacked the lithe angled presence Americans associate with the French, the one that inspires all the diet books: hers was the face and body of a lusty northern peasant in the fields, well-haunched while threshing grain to feed the village. For her own Parc Güell moment, she had encased herself in tight wide jeans, boots with a furry lined top hinting at childhood's sentimental teddy bears, and a broad-shouldered leather jacket, cracked in its seams, over which a dark blue hood flopped. I linger on the clothes because none of their pretense or faux civilized casualness did away with the strong animal presence they enhanced. She had a tremendous head of curly protoblonde hair over a broad red northern face, seamed and cracked as her jacket, teeth pretending to no special mercantilist intervention or childhood abundance, but a mouth that smiled, ready for pleasure, at her pale Spaniard.

The Spaniard escorting her was a short man with the black hair and white skin of a courtier, maybe a decade younger, also in a black jacket if one more unctuous. So considerate, so courtly in his attentions, he bestowed upon her all that some women crave from their mates: it almost took my breath away to watch the performance of such exquisite sensitivity, such fatherly attention to her every shifting discomfiture.

From the display, it seemed they had only recently met—a bar or disco? a drunken ferry ride?—and perhaps only the night before: from the way they laughed a half beat too readily, each made clear how wildly fantasies spun for both.

All this observation might sound like charlatanism of the purest order and surely some part of it is. My first job, age twelve, was to read palms with a friend in Berkeley's Walnut Square, at which age I found it strangely gratifying that adults would say, ah, really, how do you know so much about me? And perhaps such dangerous gratification, the tendrils of the potential knowing of others' realities, equips or damages a person enough that she thinks she really should travel to a place like Barcelona from which she can learn the world. That if the outer contours of identity were really that transparent, that porous, from such damage, you might be forgiven for thinking being an artist would be a good thing, the artist as code for traveler. Both carry the same thing: a curiosity about others that makes one want to take the first step out the door, because otherwise, why not stay in the contours of the self and never head to Barcelona?

You and I, we travel because of our curiosity, but is it curiosity about what the place might be or who you might become in such an imagined space?

In that endless line, the Frenchwoman basked in the attentions of her solicitous compañero. His French was enough for him to have gotten by with foreigners before, a sweet, lispingly sufficient French. Tu l'aimes le froid—? Mais si. A laugh. At any gap in their conversation, at the point into which doubt might flood, they would plug all off with a hug, a reminder of what they had known the night before: physical rapprochement their ultimate sealer. Plug it up, push it in— the tactic would work until that exact plug would no longer be sufficient.

And I kept wondering: what does he want from her?

Though it seemed clear. She traded up in one domain while he did the same in another. As Hemingway has one of his characters say, early in my friend's beloved *The Sun Also Rises*, everything is an exchange of values. In a post-austerity country, the Spaniard could use her relative wealth, mobility, or help. And she—understanding some vitality may have been lost on the altar of hedonism, lost in some plebe job—she could use some fun, all of it an equation older than Colette, going back to the time before Potiphar's wife.

She, meanwhile, was keen on asking questions about his job. He did something that required both motors and public presentation. In America he would have been a used car salesman, speaking with the assumed dignity of someone who knows others might look down on him as little more than an aid to their plans or, worse, a monkey wrench. Oui, oui, mon travail, he said, yes, my job, and then sought to clarify, briefly, particulars important only to him and his petit microcosm, not lingering, knowing with masculine instinct she probably didn't care one bit about it other than wanting to track future prospects, geographic commitments, class.

At this point I would've bet not only my place in line but also the price of my entire family's entry to Parc Güell (which seemed fairly stiff for something which Gaudí had intended as an inducement to the bourgeoisie to enjoy la naturaleza) that she had been a party girl but the party had ended seven to ten years earlier. Still not so long that she hadn't forgotten its savor. She kept glancing back at everyone behind her, with the force of an urban rat tearing into a hunk of meat in an alleyway, as if that gaze said: older, sure, but let me just enjoy this, it is mine to have. And also, a softer look after: is it such a crime? Another look at all of us behind her said: I know you are looking, and really, it is no crime, I need to have my fun, don't even cast the first stone, you have no idea how bad (monotone, subservient) the rest of my life is.

I looked elsewhere. Perhaps their age difference was greater than I'd guessed, given the scouring headlight of that gaze. That said, I strangely wanted to assure her, to enter their story: I did think it good she was having fun. Except I could not help feeling a little worried, such became my overinvolvement in her petit drama, that her Spaniard with his courtly car-selling ways was probably using her, that perhaps her mobility or whatever little sum had enabled her to bake her young skin could be enough to lift him out of hard-times Spain, out of the car lot or grease-monkey world. Oui, oui, mon travail. He wanted to be somewhere other than where he was, perhaps to be someone other, and was no different from any of us in that line at Parc Güell: travelers having come far uphill for a vision. Is it fair to say that most of the time we are all always tourists, our bodies on loan, our time to take in anything so short? And the longer we stand waiting, the shorter our time will be. Let them both travel then, in line and out, let all of us travel, let us just finally get in to our destination.

...

It seemed almost certain that with his warm eyes, not-terrible French and his extreme attentiveness he would light-finger her heart and then take some of her material belongings: this increasingly was my conclusion. They needed very little interaction, as our line caterpillared forward, about who was paying, already her purse was in hand, ready to fork forward the combined entry fee, though they would only have, like me, an hour before the sun set. He acted with supreme clarity as if he ignored the purse. While he took very seriously his position as native guide. As the line continued to snake, he kept whispering to her, or rather speaking as if in a whisper, as if only to her, about how things were proceeding: I will make this terrain plain for you.

Parc Güell, continued

The family had come uphill, we had reunited, I left my French tragedienne and her male courtesan. As a family, we strolled the last bandwidths of sun, the pathways of the upper park awaiting our entry into the lower park bedecked by Gaudí. In the upper park we heard a joyful dreadlocked ska band, saw a Serbian silhouette artist quickly cut paper profiles; as if some reminder of Pierre and me, we watched a lonely man from northern India make, with amazing skill, a rag doll belly-dance to his CD player until he sat, dejected, head in hand, at the lack of coins thrown his way. Mainly Pakistanis and northern Indians lined the upper esplanades, selling one of three things: necklaces, castanets, or themselves, defining the attraction with their narrowed range of wares as much as Spain, the park, the attraction defined all of us.

Once our hour arrived, 5:15, the time at which we could get into the lower part requiring admission, darkness swallowed most of the hill on which it perches. The distant city glimmered in the last of the day. What could we see if we only have half an hour or more before it was dark? The laundrywoman, answered a kind guard, see the salamander. The laundrywoman being a hearty stone fixture at the end of a terra-cotta wall, but as I looked at her she seemed to be weeping for us. Not far from her was splayed a mosaic salamander over which package tourists themselves splayed out in lizard fashion but one by one. Each stopped to pose, with a space of politesse carved around them, so that it would seem as if they alone had happened on a charming spot no one else had discovered.

Later in the trip I would see this exact photographic etiquette replicated on the rooftop of Gaudí's beloved La Pedrera, an apartment building commissioned by a couple, high in the bourgeoisie. The rooftop's famous chimneys and forms play against the boxlike roofs of the rest of the city, but certain refugees, heterogenous and hence lacking codes, bunched up and grumbled at the other aliens whose code stated it was a good idea to halt others from walking up and down the pathways so that the photo of a single person against the one ideal landscape could be taken, a sort of inverted Caspar David Friedrich tactic. When I look at my own photos from the visit to the Pedrera, very near the apartment in which we were staying, I see increasing disorientation. My last picture is of my thumb. Much better, in a way, to look up at the Pedrera from the street or the courtyard of the neighboring, free, and underpopulated Fundació Suñol, where you see a few unusual rooftop sentinels looking over you and also have no one's idea of the ideal spot as the antiromantic scrim over your own.

In the Parc Güell, at the salamander, the salamanders posing for the others were hoping to post their photo publicly, believing it added to the capital of their being, given that others would note their curatorial eye and unique experience.

To a fault, probably, I had never been drawn to movie stars whom everyone loved, having found perverse pride in finding beautiful what I thought the masses did not. And in this curatorial eye, there must live a double infatuation: one loves one's ability to pick up form from background, to see behind a stone, to shine a light into a neglected space.

And so, it seemed to me, was also true for my two daughters back at the Parc Güell. Too many other people had come to revel in

Gaudí; they did not want to take in any more Gaudí. No more gaud-iar, as the Spanish verb has it.

In past travels, I used to like to come to a semiarbitrary place in which I roosted, getting to know its habits, and had done this in a few locales: a village off a tobacco plantation in the mountain country of Sri Lanka, a medieval village in the Pyrenees. The serendipity of insight arising from this habit made me prefer it: more interesting salamanders seemed to crawl out from unforeseen rocks. Whereas this adult travel felt different: there were proper nouns to amass, architects to know, guidebooks to consult. And the very idea of a priori, of being a particular tourist who comes to see a specific thing for a specific reason, lacks much of the grand discovery of youth.

After ten minutes in the park, the sun still sufficient to show my youngest's face, I kneeled down with her, trying to read her mood. You want to go? I said.

It was true; she wanted to leave soon after we entered.

One definition of dramatic irony: every step you take toward your goal pushes you farther from your truest goal. And to her good credit, at seven, she saw the joke and laughed: we had come for this place, such a long trip to Barcelona, partly for her. The postcard and fantasy, the arrangements, the trip and wait, only to arrive and, ten minutes into its heart, the place released us from its spell. And why? Some imagined truer (happier, more comfortable, more alive) self awaited her anywhere but here. The irony, the irony.

We moved like victors through the sullen photographing crowd, jubilant and freed, liberated from the need to add to any quantity of hordes or the need to take in the moment. Speeding away in the cab, our driver opined warmly about the imminence of Catalunyan independence, all of us happy to free ourselves from the hordes dictating our movements.

And the French tourist and her Spaniard? Last I saw them, they leaned against a mosaic wall, trying their best in the dimming day to take, on her better phone, a selfie that would let them recall their Barcelona moment in the best light.

Speeding toward an end

There is another premise of travel that when you are about to leave a place you suddenly meet everyone interesting whom you should have met earlier.

Why should this be so? You abandon your ideas about what you came to find, you expand, and then you are fully in the place as if you are ready to die.

I only partly found the Barcelona from my pitiable-busker days, the Barcelona I thought I had known, toward the end, when I rented a bike and the bicycle let me take in the city, riding among hell-bent bicyclists who loved the cuneiform dotted into city streets and pedestrian esplanades, obeyed by locals but ignored by visitors, the bike paths a smart urban plan letting you cheerfully go all the way from the mountain to the sea or through vast swaths of mercantile enterprise while not having to push through crowds.

The man from whom I rented the bicycle had been a race-car driver but had taken over this shop which his grandfather had owned. He was surprised by the mobility of Americans: the global radar-darting across a map cannot be wholly comprehensible to someone who opens a business in a shop his grandfather has owned. After motorcars, he had decided that it was better to know the city freely, on a bicycle, and surely there was something of the adrenaline-laced motorcar-racing enterprise in biking in Barcelona, fleeing the masses while knowing yourself as part of the arteries of the city.

In that biking moment, I considered what the skateboarders knew, so serious outside the contemporary art museum in Barcelona's Raval neighborhood, a spot famous for skateboarders, such that a film was made about them: the fun of speed in a known trajectory, speed itself becoming the perception. Speed alone can be the eros, and never mind the helmetless thanatos, the bloody spill I saw one skateboarder take, or the four-year-old long-haired boarder so gung-ho on impressing his father he jumped a wall to disastrous effect.

A last note

Where is everyone going on a Sunday in Barcelona? They linger slowly, go for a walk, they go to dar un paseo, they don a beret and go for their errands. People's gazes are drawn to the stores advertising 50 percent sales after the New Year. Women wear uncomfortably high heels, young men push shopping baskets and empty strollers, and no one has very big families. This is Europe of 2015. People are having fewer children, or when they have more than one, they are poor or they had twins or they have them all at once, close to one another, to be done with it, and surely demographic data to both discount and support all this could be found.

What is it to find you no longer have Serendib, that mythical island toward which the Dutch sailed, ending up in Sri Lanka, from which the idea of serendipity comes? What is it to fix any point on the map? Perhaps this is what Elizabeth Bishop means when she talks about being in one place, thinking of there instead of getting here. We must have a biological urge to retain an illusion of Valhalla, to keep escape our option, even if here be dragons.

To bring my family here meant, in a sense, to slay that girl who had been an earnest dreamy busker outside that cathedral with that French trompettiste. To show them something of the old, to induct the next generation into the charms of travel. My older daughter, eleven, loved walking anywhere, and then stopping to choose tapas or a croissant, imagining a future life that would include only these elements: walking, exploring, eating. My younger daughter found elements of travel overwhelming, especially the crowds that made one-on-one perception harder. Perhaps part of returning to a place is that you discover how much less self-infatuated you are than when you were all blind potential.

I write this from the Fifth Avenue of Barcelona, not far from La Pedrera, with only a few more days to go before returning home. The faces of the Barcelonans, walking by in pairs as if exiled from

Noah's boat and forced into lives of endless consumption, getting and spending, look weary, but at least they are together: in this city they understand not only walking but also the beauty of walking together. Spanish men and Japanese women, a common pairing, pass by: it is, as Robert Hughes fulminates in his magisterial, cranky book, a city taken over by Californian and Japanese tastes.

Mothers and daughters wear identical boots. One mother strokes her daughter's vest, produced by sweat factories in Asia. Dogs, humorous and spotted, drag owners along. Servitude to the bourgeois ideal, to *Kinder, Küche, Kirche* far from the madding crowd, surrounds me. People do not treat children here with southern warmth but more with the watchful, warm regard you might have toward a particular investment: often parents walk by, anxious but purposely unheeding as a child cries behind them. These children study their parents for cues, while waiters watchful for more business, wearing jeans originally fashioned in San Francisco at the time of the gold rush, try luring the unheeding parents in for an adult café. Everyone has a phone and an attitude toward bags and belongings.

This is a neighborhood which sees people having a lonely air at night as they let themselves into their apartment buildings hung with tasteful art. Certain hours bring unhappiness, people trying to find succor. They belong, they don't question, but they are exhausted from enjoyment while trying to move ahead. In luxurious neighborhoods, signs of Europe's austerity measures are inverted but somehow live on in body parts: on display in the length of a women's legs, paraded in elaborate tights, or proudly displayed in boots and fetish objects. Couples comfortable with each other still have lots of opining and creature comforts to share within themselves and with other couples: you very much feel Marx's idea of the bourgeois in this part of Barcelona, where you do not find package tours but you find the urban French, those coming to seek in their travels, so often, a place similar to home.

At a local exhibit of the photographer Salgado, people bunched up to look at the Kuikuros' monkey-spine photos, Salgado showing us the extreme areas of the earth where the details vary, but as the gallery-goers left, in their self-satisfied, weary faces sizzled the death of dreams. If you talk with them, they are unfailingly present, helpful, but the friendliness has its boundaries. And yet what was it, after all, that I was trying to induct my children into?

A true final thought

In my last sight of Pierre the busker, he was awake in my bed, shirtless and smiling like a smaller Jean-Paul Belmondo. I was leaving for the day; we would meet up later; I think I was answering some message from the publicidad agency. Faites comme vous êtes chez vous, he said jokingly before I left, feel at home. We had not slept together, we had merely slept next to each other, compañeros of the camino, fellow buskers, followers of separate romantic myths, survivors of La Catedral, talking all night. When I came back a few hours later, he was gone, as was the camera my father had given me and perhaps some other important items.

What had he robbed me of? Is it not always safer to have stayed home and thought of here? There was nowhere to send that bolus of violence, the asymmetry of the letter his theft sent me. I fled then, late in the day, heading to the train station. I took the train partway to Annecy, which would have been his next destination, and then turned back. I would never reach Annecy and its beautiful lake, as I would never reach many beautiful places: Should I have stayed in them and thought of home? Instead I went on to follow the more organized idea of the rest of the summer, the green, taking the boat to Cork, making my way through crowds filling the streets for a U2 concert, and from there to Yeats' grave in Sligo, keeping the Barcelona I knew a similarly buried memory. What burial song could accompany the loss of the romantic dream?

In an alleyway on my truly last day, just outside the cabinet of curiosities near the Catedral, a museum of solicitude, a guitar player named Justi with a saddened wise way about him and a cheerful sax player from Mexico City do what they can to sing Justi's songs into a mic.

Up the cobblestoned street comes a gypsy girl in socks with great glee and a not-terrible voice. She takes over the mic which harmonizes a tone one third above her voice and, so augmented, she belts out the chorus of a dispensable pop anthem while Justi and his Mexican accompanist smile, trying to silence her with grace, as now they can take up public space solely by dispensation of the town's bureaucracy, which has started to assign buskers two-hour intervals. And the gypsy girl with her libido for song could ruin it for Justi and his pal, because she cannot just sing into the mic but must do so loudly, her song of self. Clearly this exact charade has been enacted plenty of times: she has them and their polite smiles do little to fend her off. How come you don't let me sing with you? she keeps saying, just a little. Like all of us, she wants that interpenetration of realms that a port city allows: gypsy become busker become tourist with family. But she must stay in her role, their kind firmness succeeds in shushing her, while the cabinet of curiosities museum and its oversolicitous guards await me. Long before the guards think it appropriate, I flee the museum, which, with an enchanting but overwhelming collection, makes me drown in the stuff of Barcelona. As I walk back out into that square emptied of Justi, his sax-player, the bestockinged gypsy girl, this last day returns Barcelona to me: the perverse cheer of travel for which there is no real guidebook. First you must pass the chaos of uninvited loudness before entering an enclave of the professionally overfriendly. As you head through an open passageway, admire the last of the day's light slanting. So that you might again appreciate the generosity of travel, note that some random mute might sidle right up to you: toothless, he wants to hand you a paper napkin folded into a rose, with, this time, no coin needed. Inside the rose the questions: to travel well, must you leave behind the self you thought you were coming to see? Once you had within you someone who knew how to appreciate, to live in the moment, walking to see the sea, someone who thought less and lived more. Is Serendib the place where the dragons in the corner of the map assault you most with questions about the self? Is our greatest travel the one we make through time?

Forget the mute beggar. As Bishop asks: Why, why must we have our dreams and also fulfill them? Stay naked for one more second. Is it not enough just to have the dream? Take Barcelona.

DAUGHTER OF CALIFORNIA

Is there no change of death in paradise?
—Wallace Stevens

Pitch dirt onto a parent's dead body and in that second understand that bits of dirt just became as much part of the parent as any other bit you might hold onto: a snapshot, a clock with bent hands, shoes still bearing the imprint of feet, ties scented with stale aspiration. We mortals grasp. In my father's last minute as a living, breathing, incorporated entity, he was on the phone with me—or rather a nurse I'll call Bob held the phone up to my father's ear.

Before my last conversation with my father last September, the first of many unilateral discussions ever since, I had fallen asleep next to my three-year-old, helping her get to bed, a custom probably far too common in our house with its tilt toward entropy.

This house: it is situated in the kind of town for which Manhattanites leave the grid. Faces radiant, they come to trip over our uneven sidewalks, aquiver with the possibility of serendipity and rustication. Obedient to hebdomadal divisions, they rise for their upstate sabbath fully pagan, rousting in ancient corporeal nostalgia: antiques and wine, jam, farmers' markets, holiday festivals, round bread, any ritual useful in making sense of time, not to mention the oddity of toting around a body bearing desire and all its malfunctions.

My father, a geophysicist, would have remarked less on the Manhattan tourists and more on the old granite of upstate New York, its igneous intrusive, so different from the endless metamorphic slop and shift of soft Californian plates in which sections of oceanside cliff change overnight, where if a tsunami won't get you, a shark will.

This same scientist once stood in his office, an old, almost condemned Art Deco building in an Oakland not yet refurbished by Jerry Brown's idealism. Under and around him the great earthquake of 1989 terrorized the earth. In a building not up to code in its seismic retrofitting, there my father stood under an antique chandelier and not under a doorframe as all Californian schoolchildren learn to do early in primary school, nor under a desk or table, but keeping his balance on the rolling earth.

From timing the swings of that potentially lethal lamp, my father factored the P and S waves on the surface of the land and in this way estimated the geographic navel of the earthquake, its epicenter. Later he was pleased not so much to have survived without a scratch, given that the quake figured 6.9 on the Richter scale and caused scads of devastation, but rather more tickled that his knowledge of California fault lines and mathematics had positioned the epicenter accurately, some fifty-six miles away on the coast of Santa Cruz.

The night of his death, while half sleeping in New York, the night that started a period of not just unilateral conversation but unknowable maps, I heard my husband say: I got a call. Your father's dying. This time it's real.

For years this father, half bon vivant and half scientist, had been creeping farther and farther out onto an isthmus of abstraction. I found it easiest to understand the clouds that increasingly populated his watery blue eyes and his similarly aqueous mind as some brilliant philter the body seeped into one's brain as a way to soften the fear of dying.

My father loved putting on a brave show. Despite his early years in Israel that had made him a chalutznik, yet another pioneer taught that men should sport only fur but no sensitivity, like all of us he had his favorite talismans against fear and the frequency of their apparition could show even a casual observer how afraid he really was. His military posture, for one, with its rigid grace, which made his bearded self look at, say, a party—this was a man who loved parties—like a blue-eyed Lincoln reconfigured as your average broad-shouldered lieutenant. He would sit smiling and upright as if to say: I am here, I claim this spot on the mobile earth, nothing threatens me, I am ready for pleasure.

Another talisman against fear would be one of his favorite morning songs, a kabbalistic melody whose words, translated from Hebrew, told him that *all the world is a narrow bridge, and the most important thing is not to fear (the passage from life to death).* In his long, stretched-out dying, he showed a survivor's tenacity, his final talisman: if theoretically he wanted to die, in reality he found it hard to leave the party.

We the living become quick adepts in our trafficking in the jargon of meds which, in our modern-day business of dying, act as a professional undertaker, fake in their helpfulness, words that slither and whisper and prompt us alongside our slow processionals toward a funeral.

Or you could say we become a kind of snake swallowing the elephant of death, à la the illustration in the early pages of *The Little Prince* which shows the elephant bulging inside the boa constrictor.

Therefore, to use the jargon our family so obediently swallowed: for months prior to the flash and siren of the last ambulance taking him to the last hospital, my father could be found in a *skilled nursing facility*, an infelicitous phrase which always made me wonder, what, as opposed to that other facility known for its staff so judiciously unskilled?

In his non-home, attended to by those with skills, he had been lying in bed or in a wheelchair playing pioneer tunes on his harmonica in desultory fashion near the nurses' station, positioned on an island which was a decommissioned naval base out in northern California. Could it have been more perfect that the name of his home, dedicated to liminal states, was Water's Edge?

What I tried to understand that mapless last night of his life was that this time his dying was real. From our entropic New York aerie, this was the totality of what I could divine.

I sat in our tiny dining room next to my husband who was dialing the hospital and using his best Brooklyn-bred diplomacy to get through the telephone lines into the exact right artery that would lead into the ER and whatever last bit of listening might be left in my father's ear.

I should say that I sat like a penitent schoolgirl, fists clenched between tight knees, waiting in a room that had just lost its circulation. I chilled, for once the phrase right, since the temperature of the world had just dropped. While we tried getting through, it seemed everyone else in my family also tried the lines, this being a family not known for its lack of words. Of course at this second the lines would be getting clogged, heart to head, family flocking to its cerebral patriarch, and in seconds I would lose the chance to—to do what? Use words to sustain a last moment? Did the urgency of needing to talk to him have to do with affirming our connection? To say life and all its recent indignities had mattered? To show that despite being geographically challenged I would care and then care always, memory conjugated out over the rest of my lifetime? I cared, I care, I will care, those who don't know you will care, you have a legacy.

Before those crucial seven ounces of consciousness left his body, I had to tell him he mattered, that all of the suffering and aspiration of his life had been worthwhile, that we mattered, that he would continue to matter within the context of the living.

Since the dawn of the answering machine, I have been a phone-phobe, voice seeming such a poor substitute for presence. This unfortunate sensibility makes me lack the grace of friends who sound ready and delighted to answer a ring, those with the talent of making time expand accordionlike in their affinity with Bell's invention. Instead, and this serves as no apologia, I seem always to hang up first, caveman-like, unrefined and coarse: there should be a twelve-step program for those like me. Hi, I'm Edie and I do bad phone. If email redeemed most of my social life, which it did, my aversion to the phone stood as one of many traits which my father, with his open attitude but his unfamiliarity with computerized letters, accepted as a quirk.

Simply, therefore, in that pendulous minute before I could talk with my father, my job was, once again, to try to make the phone a friend. It was all I had.

My husband handed me the receiver and Bob the nurse came on to say: You want to say your goodbyes.

Right, I thought in that nanosecond, brilliant, that's the name for it, I'm going to say my goodbyes.

The plural fit for a man of my father's complexity, suspended in a metaphysical state of so many parts, within a state of so many pluralities.

And until that moment I had not realized that every person has, stored within, some finite amount of goodbyes for each person who matters and that right now, despite all brink moments and prior goodbyes, I was about to use up the last goodbye, tagged for him alone. This time the goodbye reverted to a greater status. I was about to spend my last goodbye as if some maximum leader had just declared the currency of goodbye not debased by all its manifold apparitions. This time the currency would *count.*

For five years, all my father's near deaths had summoned me from New York back to California. Each death seemed realer than the one that came before. Each time my father's Egyptian lady doctor said to me, *If it were my dad I'd come now.* Westward I flew, often with a baby on my lap, and the babies grew. The youngest especially became a fan of fire trucks, given the coincidence of their hectic arrival, coming to oxygenate her grandfather every second day after we arrived for a visit to California.

There he would be, in his medically outfitted room off the kitchen on the lower level of my parents' house, his heart exalted by the nearness of family but his lungs drowning in the fluid that kept wanting to fill that aqueous spirit, and once again we would be summoning empirical data and conventional logic in order to persuade the scientist, the traveler who now wanted to stay home, that this was something of an emergency. There I would be, fingers robotic in dialing 911 for the firemen to come again—I got to know them—up the fifty-one stairs to the house in order to put yet another oxygen mask on him and spirit him away and me into the plethora of questions that came in his wake, all from the young truck-lover (who now every night, her choice, her subliminal Yahrzeit, sleeps in a plastic replica of all those fire trucks):

Where do the firemen take him? Why does Saba wear that mask? Will they fix Saba so he can walk again?

And my own questions, all mainly circulating around one: Did he not once get me to promise that his life's coda would have the dignity of freedom he had found in his adopted state? But who was not to say that in his travels, bedbound, he was not fulfilling the imaginative promise of California?

Consider the name. Unlike other states drawn from Spanish—Colorado ("red"), Florida ("flowered"), Nevada ("snowy")—the name California itself is drawn from a fantasy land mentioned in *Don Quixote*, and before that a different land imagined in a chivalric romance by Rodríguez de Montalvo. Which suggests how readily you, too, can project on a land made up of such shifting plates. It is a shock to encounter, say, a tenth-generation Californian—though they do exist, great-grandchildren of dusty legacy and agricultural ingenuity, often the great-grandsons of early ranchers with some Mexican or Spanish romance thrown in.

Consider that whenever America encountered problems with coexistence, which sounds better in Spanish, *convivencia*, it expanded its territories westward, so that a slow seep of individualism spread from the tight eastern harbors out toward the hyperindividualism of the west, which may go a long way toward explaining why people from the middle states tend to be so other-directed and polite, a legacy of making do enough to declare, as in the license plates of Oklahoma, hey, this state is okay.

Whereas, in order to feel their own state is okay, citizens of California must perform elaborate tricks, yogic, Buddhist or from some other polyverse. To California they come to go beyond the quais of okayness, to find their big dreams, seeing it as Don Quixote might: the state will be a kindly queen, allowing them to realize, in acreage and billboards, their fantasies.

This was how my father, a resourceful, adaptable person, well suited in psyche and profession to the state, used it. An ambitious restless geophysicist, he was dedicated to, as one of his company's business cards had it, *the evaluation and exploration of natural resources*.

Part of the liberty of the state, of course, has to do with the weather: it rarely constrains you, and when it does, the constraint has the dimensions of a Greek tragedy, as only the biggest ecological disasters set foot here: earthquakes, tsunamis, mudslides, fires, geological capstones fitting the dimensions of the state, the heroic flaws and grand destinies of those drawn to it. If every state has a psychological age appropriate to it, California is forever an adolescent, dreaming in bright colors and assuming suicidal proportions at its misfortunes.

Which may be one of the reasons, right before we moved into its take-all-comers embrace, the state assumed leadership in that youngest of decades, the sixties: the civil rights movement, the free speech movement, the rollicking music, and the rocking hills of Haight-Ashbury all fit the national demographic bulge of youth. Accordingly, the majority of my friends' parents came from the following range, one drawn from the disappointed dreams of youth: drifters, horse-race gamblers, Vietnam vets, café chess players, social agitators, drug users, therapists, famous musicians, polyamorists or ex–psych ward types.

Many were divorced or separated or lived in alternative arrangements. By contrast my family seemed solid and well endowed, conventional, with two working parents, their indiscretions unknown. California and the times may not have made much of a dent in my parents' Old World creamed herring and Mediterranean tomato-cucumber-lemon-onion diet, but it did allow them to wear peasant shirts from my father's many travels at all the many parties they hosted, parties in which my mother, an engineer at the public transit system, would invariably at some point don her green jeweled belly-dance outfit to shimmy before the guests, ululating as she had taught many of them to do, often accompanied by the happy jiggling students she also taught in a swirl of cloths on Sunday mornings, all before she invited my father up to do a sort of loose-hipped sheikh imitation with her before all of them: California at its multiethnic apotheosis.

Come to the party and we'll dance for you!

The one common social denominator in any setting was this: the body, its hopes, its staving off of decay.

My response to this awareness of social disparity—all that we seemed to have in relation to all others seemed to lack—was to try to bring people in to what seemed the potluck bounty of our house, and even without my intervention, an uncountable many came and lived with us. A friend and her confused mother; the daughter of a pot-smoking vet who later became something of a celebrity murderer; a German exchange student; a polarity therapist; a secretary; a massage therapist; a lost philosopher; a friend with stepmother troubles; a friend with stepfather troubles. The list goes on. Beyond the guests, a succession of people lived in the dank basement apartment, and one had an ex-boyfriend who came by, parking his red-painted former milk truck on our cul-de-sac for a week. I would bring him treats until I finally asked my parents if he too could not live in the house, one that had been bought for $25,000 back when that area of South Berkeley, not far from the invisible but real border with Oakland, was considered too close to racial troubles. In our basement kitchen, this latest of our inhabitants penned for his dented guitar a song that ricochets around my head sometimes, a Californian anthem with one of those strident melodies of childhood:

I'm a drifter and I drift this world around
And I know who I want to be and just where I've been
To be free to flow with the wind.

And despite or because of all its disappointed dreaming drifters, the town seemed to function, believing itself a microcosm of the world, the best of the best to be found there, believing itself potent on the world stage. Alice Waters was starting Chez Panisse, the gourmet ghetto mentality of the town was radiating out, the town was claiming its position as the only American city to have its own foreign policy and my father's grandiosity linked with the town's.

Just as, after being a shepherd studying sheep husbandry, my father abandoned pastoral charms to go bigger, mastering geothermal energy as a means, in his view, to save the world, every family trip we ever took abandoned pleasure and instead involved long pilgrimages to sulfurous, spitting sections of the earth where the grandeur of nature dwarfed us. In relaxation, my father, and hence our family, never proved lazy.

Even after the fog of dementia started to pour in, even as he started his long slow dying, I would, as ever, try to make the phone a friend and call him. If I asked how he was doing, he might say: Well, some medieval colleagues and I were trying to figure out all the names of God and the colleagues were really quite congenial. Or: Someone handed me a capsule containing a worm that could destroy humanity and I was just figuring out the best way to save everyone.

Like the small liberal town he had chosen, he'd had a long-term utopian mission to save the world. He had started an Israeli cultural circle and would invite prominent Bedouins, Palestinians, and Arabs to come speak to a volatile group of talkers. He supported causes, soup kitchens, candidates. The Department of Energy named him, with great ceremony and a placard, an energy pioneer. He did what he could in his way, writing a poem that appeared in a millennial anthology, *Prayers for a Thousand Years*, that had a last line that went something like this: May I in my small way do the best I can, knowing that for my time I did the best I could for others.

And for all his love of trafficking with high and mighty causes, people, places, he remained a socialist, a person who wore the same holey plaid shirts, who would say, if a vase broke: It's just a thing. He never went out without a roll of quarters in one of his threadbare pockets, ready to dispense change to people in need. He was unafraid of homeless people found sleeping in his car and would give them a ride wherever they needed. When at age fourteen I was caught stealing sunglasses for my brother's birthday, from a drugstore on Telegraph Avenue, the open-air post-hippie emporium street that hosted so many lost denizens, under the influence of all those friends the products of those broken post-sixties Californian homes, my father did not scold me. Instead he merely shook his head, hours after my release from a scary graffitied cell, and said: Look, Edie, it's never the thing that counts when you give a gift, it is the thought. Thought is everything.

In later life, accordingly, he inhabited his body as if thought were everything, the body an uneasy, stolen perch, an afterthought, a car in which his homeless self happened to find itself. Once, on a business trip while I was living on the Upper West Side, he visited me and said goodbye to me on Broadway. I watched him walk away, his back disappearing into the sidewalk masses. A father barely skimming the earth, he carried not even a briefcase, a stick-skinny man whose movement radiated out from a loose central axis, wrists flopping out a bit as if the wind could spirit him and his untailored suit away.

Sometimes, during my father's long dying, our upstate–New York family flew west to spend some summer month in one housesitting situation or another, caring for this canary or that dog, my daughters delighted to be in the ease of extended family and the weather that surrounded them. Their sociable grandfather, who had always had a bipolar way of saying goodbye—either expert in the gooey and endless Jewish art of goodbye, or Israeli in the way he could say, for example, to someone he was chauffeuring, I love you, now get out!—would be equally delighted by the multiplication of family.

His party never ended, the goodbyes never stopped, and meanwhile the meds worked their damage, fighting a war in his liver, the meds that said to his corporeal being, essentially, the opposite of *I love you, now get out!*

I destroy you; now you must stay in life!

A few months after my father's death, the attending doctor described Bob, the last person in that last room, as a kind and dedicated representative of the art of nursing, a practice for which I only gain respect each passing year of my own life as a two-time mother and undifferentiated mortal.

There Bob was, on the phone in that expanse of time, his voice so dry and tight it almost sounded sarcastic, conveying over the unclotted line the atmosphere of the emergency room, thick with death, telling me: You want to say your goodbyes.

Yes? I said.

You can talk, he can hear you, he said.

He could hear but could he listen? Back to the character of this father of mine. In the same way that I was living in exile, out in New York, forever hankering for the calm skies of my northern Californian childhood, the freedom of being able to go outdoors with your children any time you darn well chose, my father had lived his whole life in exile. We grew up in a little Israel of the imagination, set, provisionally, in the liberal airs of Berkeley. My father's Israel had begun in 1933, where he had moved when he was three. Prior to that, his family had lived in the small Polish town of Przmsl where his father, Joshua, had been a woodsman and a community leader. When anti-Semitism roved their town like some fanged beast, Joshua scented survival and took his family to Haifa. Soon after, all the family—the uncles and grandfathers and cousins who remained in Poland—were killed. Survival instinct, therefore, lived deep in the nature or nurture of the family.

Someone who married into the Meidavs traced our genealogy back point by diasporic point through the Maharal of Prague, the Baal Shem Tov and Rashi, through Lucca, Italy, through the house of David and all the way back to some humble Palestinian second-century-BCE sandalmaker named Yohanan, and something about this millennial-long connection to the land paradoxically provided succor to my increasingly leftist father who loved the ideation of the Palestinian thinker Sari Nusseibeh. To his death, this American exile remained an exponent of the two-state solution, clearly a *yored*, a person who had "come down from" Israel, a distant survivor of an era and not, as our Israeli cousins liked to point out, a person on the ground, like his more rightist brother who had remained in Haifa.

Part of my father's lofty idealism—so well suited to both California and his Israel of the 1950s, before a moral conscience started riddling certain sectors—meant that a favorite book among the many antique books in his collections was a set of lithographs done by David Roberts, *Travels to the Holy Land*, in which the Englishman had penned lovely romanticizing images of Bedouins hunkered down by a well, little aquarelle-like images of the land and its peoples coexisting, and for copies of books such as these, preserving the memory of a time before strife, my father would travel to book fairs seeking out unfoxed copies of the early Holy Land.

In this way and in so many others, my father was ideally suited to California. Because California seems to listen but insists on rose-colored landscapes. It has the compelling charisma of a narcissist, one which lures emigrants out to fulfill internal, narcissistic dictates. In its royal beneficence it makes lifestyle urges, ethical or sybaritic, holy, the body its temple.

...

Stay simple, a handwritten imperative on the cover of a notebook that one of our Berkeley house's many inmates dictated. Stay simple, an idea perplexing my child's mind. Was it better to stay simple so one could feel the world and all its categories better, anew, as if one were truly an innocent? Or was it better to gain in the intricacies of the world, cultural or natural, so that one could better understand its phenomena? Is it better to know the name of a leaf or does knowing the name mask appreciation of the leaf?

If you could, hypothetically, wash yourself clean of culture, would you then live the life of the body more purely? Our California had all the romantic-savage idealism of Truffaut's *The Wild Child*, in which the wolf-boy loses the inner truth of his body once he is civilized, yet our California also had the gourmet jadedness of your average American international food court: sample the best of everywhere else, become a multiplied citizen, and why ever leave? Motion could become stasis in the perfect microcosm of Berkeley.

We came to the Zion of California, and specifically Berkeley, after my family had already tried out Saint Louis, Haifa, Toronto, Westbury. We came the year the sixties truly ended, that is, in 1974, when the whole city was entering what I would later realize was one prolonged hangover, the buzzkill that included Reagan, the Charles Manson years, the various propositions announcing that people did not want to pay taxes to support anyone other than themselves. Vietnam veterans smoked their only pleasant artifacts of the war, their tiny pinched hoardables, sitting on the curbs along Telegraph Avenue, the main drag toward the university, steeping the whole area in sickly sweet fumes. Open-air sellers sold hippie jewelry—and what did ever happen to macramé, which seemed such an important art to my young self, as important as basket weaving or the making of incense holders?—underneath a mural depicting the people's struggle to save People's Park from the pigs, the police. There was a sense of revolution mutely dimmed. Now the bourgeoisie got to eat their massive alfalfa-sprout salads while kids growing up during that time in that place got to see what happened if you went the way of drugs, a massive cautionary display on every corner.

So in the end the body became the path of improvement.

California's adolescent desire to make a better world, once nipped, became the realpolitik of someone entering their late twenties and early thirties, the more mature evaluation made by someone who realizes their own risks and mortality and who then makes adjustments.

In the buzzkill years, seeded by a genealogy beginning with the Jack LaLannes and continued by the Jane Fondas, what the state's citizens were left with was the body. In the state I grew up in, the body was everything. You could retreat into the body and its nurturance and rejuvenation, its vitamin protocol or cryogenic suspension. Retreat into a fanfold of body therapies because the body would not betray, or if it did, it was your fault. You could control your health, as well as your fate, and any illness was a sign of poor internal combustion. Every adult I knew was dedicated toward some form of self-development, and these forms usually radiated from and toward the body.

From northern California all these body therapies—what we could see from another vantage as focused outcomes of the gold rush—were introduced, refined, reified, consolidated. Trager points, polarity, dance continuum, Rolfing, tai chi. Because, finally, when you had renounced your birthright, when politics had betrayed you, when you could not believe in your dreams, in community or connection or culture, you would always have the body, its urges, and the sophrosyne of the state writ upon it. You could endlessly self-improve, climb fire trails, eat more phytonutrients, meditate for hours a day and thus insure your own longevity or at least your survival when the great cataclysms would come, and bet your earthquake insurance come they would.

On the east coast and perhaps everywhere else, when people find a body therapy they like, they cling to it as if it is a splintered board after a shipwreck, singular and intense in their devotion to it, truly zealous acolytes in crowded corridors in Manhattan or in meetings in little hard-to-find restaurants. But on the west coast, people slip in and out of the ever-present therapies—because to survive in a place that doesn't squeeze your contours with a social contract as, say, with New England's lawns and flags, you need to have some kind of pressure around your corporeal self—with an ease and blending akin to all the state's experiments with pineapple and pimiento: California Pizza Kitchen indeed.

My parents were not wholly immune to these new-fangled body therapies but also, interestingly, managed to remain in a prior century. My mother used olive oil on her face; on his hair my father used a tube of 1950s grease, part of a storm-cloud gathering of intention prior to any important business meeting. Of course he had other icons, all bespeaking the dream of ultimate mobility: the cologne of departure, the briefcase, the traveler's Dopp kit with its tweezers, Band-Aids, scissors, shoe polish, an open briefcase. Most of my father's life was spent in movement. When I was young, he would travel for months at a time for the United Nations to develop sustainable energy projects in Ethiopia, Honduras, Kenya, the Philippines, and who knows where else.

My favorite memory of him from my kindergarten years is of a card he sent to me in his careful, floral immigrant cursive, a bird's African feathers tufted on the front. In his absence, like our last phone call, the token became everything.

After his brief stint for the UN, where he couldn't stand being a government man, out in California, the land of possibility and future attainment, he started two companies. Over his career, he traveled the world but only after his death, as I took the plane westward that chilly middle of the night, did I realize that on planes, trains, boats, in any movement, I had always been closest to him.

A few months after his death, I went on an already-planned research trip to Nicaragua and realized, as the plane began its touchdown in Managua, the local women around me busily applying eye makeup against the backdrop of volcanoes, how so many moments of his life were spent in true California sybaritic fashion, enjoying and appreciating the artistry of the people around him, a man unpretentious in wishing to connect with all he met, parking attendant or fellow passenger, always filled with stories of savoring the lives of strangers: an older woman whose charity in Nicaragua he wished to help, some Oakland evangelist whose family needed succor, as well as the occasional dignitary or billionaire. He may have reserved his greatest fondness, however, for the chef at the Hotel Cesar in Managua.

Ten years before he died, five before his mind started its continental drift, he invited me to come translate on a business trip: we'd use the Hotel Cesar as our base. As with any Californian doing tai chi in the sun, he justified pleasure if it fell in the service of utopian work. Blithe about risk, the kind of person who had fallen down elevator shafts, into hot springs, and down stairs around the world, he wanted to share the pleasures of the Cesar. Never mind that on that first Nicaragua trip, I ended up having a life-or-death experience in the jungle when he sent me packing on laden burros up the volcano Momotombo with a team of brothers. Using machetes to cut the jungle ahead, the brothers and I were to find spots to place antiquated iron boxes containing seismic monitors: if it formed part of the strategy that the brothers lost the youngest brother who didn't know the volcano, that the dark tugged in around the youngest and me, my father could not have known. Nor could he have guessed that, upon realizing our fate, this boy turned upon me with his own burning question: Why is it American girls don't like Nicaraguan boys? Tramping through unknown wilderness, sharing my last water, we ended up clinging to one tree, our burros tied up below, skittish. While the nighttime cobras hissed below us, the young brother persisted in wanting to lose his virginity, the longest night of my life, and only by some instinct I cannot find or locate now, I led us the next morning toward what became eventually a path and a road and we were finally found.

Only that I was perplexed anew by my father, who, upon my return back to him and his Hotel Cesar, sighed, relieved, his accent thicker than ever: *I'm so glad I did not know you were lost, that I had no clue it was happening!* And why not? *I would have tried to send helicopters to try to rescue you!* Hopeful ignorance thus triumphed over friction, a possibly Israeli trait which also suited him to California, the state of mind in which people pursue the specificities of lifestyle, each person facing the ocean, rather than be too aware of the particularities of those who rub shoulders nearby.

During that first visit to Nicaragua, he and I stayed a few more days at the Hotel Cesar where with the chef and others he chatted, a bit like Hemingway in Cuba if without the drink, happy to sit poolside, speaking an intelligible if slow Spanish to one person after another in business meetings filled in equal parts with charm and futility. His Nicaraguan ventures, motivated by a typically idealistic desire to provide what he thought was a sustainable clean energy source to people in need, never thrived. Part of this failure, as one associate later told me, had to do with his refusal to adhere to important local customs, bribery paramount among them. And clinging to some self-spun philosophy, his imagined fortunes rose and sank in a second like those of a dreamy 1849 gold miner.

Prospecting for something more incorporeal, when I came for the second time to Nicaragua, soon after his death, I was glad to stay anywhere but in the ache of his memory, staying not in the Cesar but in a tatty little inn. Like him, I had to rely hugely on the kindness of strangers and so felt especially close to him, a father who made random new acquaintances his mobile family, much like our California and much like his profession, which converted the chance of steam into an impermanent, aspirational project. What he bequeathed me: to be in exile, making only of the body and one's immediate acquaintances a home.

His most religious custom was to check into a hotel in some foreign city and then call my mother at home to say he had reached his latest geographical coordinates: the tenacity had arrived at its goal, and in this, my parents accorded each other great latitude. In movement—the dream shared by Zion and California—one could find meaning, purpose, belonging.

Say your goodbyes then, said Bob the unflappable nurse.

In other words, make a cord to a man of so many moveable parts.

In that one last second I had to talk to him—fittingly exiled—the trumpet-blast of a lifetime together came out of me:

Dad, I said, never having had the right name to call him, you are responsible for so much of anything that is good in me and your children and grandchildren love you and we'll do what we can to honor your memory and legacy and all the good you've sown and you've been holding on so long and now it might be your time to let go and do you remember that song you loved about all the world being a narrow bridge, the important thing being not to fear and—

I got to hang up now, said Bob the knowledgeable, sixty seconds into my swan song.

Thirty seconds later, according to later reportage, my father, who allegedly smiled and nodded lightly as I spoke, was dead.

No one gives you a user manual for such moments. Somewhere inside I had signed a contract that I would be by my father's side when he died, a kind of fellow traveler, as if my childhood in Berkeley—that made-up Californian confection, a pastiche of a bardo, made up of everyone else's in-between spaces, a kind of tunnel—meant I had to be with him in this final threshold zone.

That we had that last moment could have relieved me, just as my father was relieved not to have sent helicopters to rescue me from near death in that Nicaraguan jungle. To be close but not to have to feel the pain of potential separation.

I could have said: Jeez, at least I got to talk to my dad in his last second. He heard me, he smiled.

Instead, when a minute later the doctor called us in New York to tell us what we already knew, I felt I had betrayed my father's legacy by not being by his side, that I had taken his California Zion lesson too deeply and become a person too much in movement, too much a traveler, too far away, following dreams of my own.

And still that doctor's call released me from a deep freeze. I ran through our house as if on amphetamines, middle of the night on tiptoes, unable not to rush, as if it would change anything if I were speedy in booking a ticket from Albany, the nearest airport, so I could fly toward California. We the living scurry while our dead have all the time in the world. History sleeps; we hurry toward our ends. Plus I did not want to wake my kids to say I was going. Their relative innocence, lips fluttering over dream-words, seemed crucial, almost more important than whatever had just happened. This was how my psyche compartmentalized loss. If you don't orphan details, you won't have to see your own orphaning.

In a cold car in a parking lot in the middle of the night at that Albany airport, I pretended to sleep before my flight, enjoying the physical discomfort. No bed of nails could have been spiky enough. Already in movement I was closer to him but still I needed a physical correlate to the metaphysical dislodging death performs, some way to show my father I understood what his body might have known, despite its hypersedation, in all its recent injustices.

When I got to California, it felt oddly fitting that the religious mandates around his burial kept me from seeing his body on that first day, a decent veil. My siblings and I sat outside the back door of the locked, squat suburban building within which a guard sat praying over his body. We looked past native wildflowers into a valley half river-rift and half tectonic shift, with a large silver aqueduct lacking, given the drought, the life-force of water roaring down into the canyon: exactly the kind of landscape my father would have appreciated, one where the grandeur of nature dwarfed a small token of human intervention, your archetypal Californian scene.

The next day, I sat in a room in that squat building alone with his body, so oddly still and yet alive, his huge bony head looking peaceful, the love that he radiated out to so many chillingly present in the room.

My youngest daughter, the fire truck lover, the three-year-old who has something of my father's brow, had told me that morning she had glimpsed Saba walking in the house again and that, scared, she had hidden from him. The night of his death, before we knew he was dying, before we put her to sleep in that upstate house with its tilt toward entropic custom, she had been trying to tell me, with strange insistence, that sometimes people go to hospitals and never leave. With adult casualness, I had considered her talk merely the metabolism of some discussion she'd overheard a month earlier.

Though in retrospect, signs collected: earlier that September day, in the first of two classes I taught, I'd repressed the urge to share an anecdote on radical shifts in perception, not telling students the story of the hallucinatory airport moment in which I'd learned a beloved great-uncle had died, when around me flight-goers no longer were sleepwalkers but keenly aware each act made a necessary but ludicrous feint against the overwhelming heaviness of mortality. The next class I taught, I similarly had to avoid laughing uncontrollably, much as I'd done at the exact moment a best friend of mine was killed miles away from where I sat in a classroom as a high school student in a troubled Jerusalem.

Perhaps these facts—my daughter's insistence on the suddenness of death, the odd telegraphs I wanted to convey to my students but did not—were circumstantial or are as strong as the telephone cord. What ties the living to the dead, after a while, has mostly to do with the cord of belief, while the soul of writing will always be elegy: one uses words to create a trail back to some missing source, the platonic home you hope for but can never quite reach. Like the hundreds of unfinished highways you find in California, founded on big dreams and crashing in reality, all the roads that begin, continue, and never reach their ends, this bit of writing is, perhaps necessarily, unilateral, incapable of neat conclusion.

I write this from the lobby of a Cuban hotel in the spring of 2011 under a statue of the one omnipresent heroic American you find here,

Lincoln, the emaciated liberator, almost as ubiquitous as Che or Fidel, Bolivar, Allende, Maceo, Martí. My family, daughters and all, have been living in this country in an apartment owned by a slumlord on a street spilling over occasionally with rivers of sewage. For days at a time, we will have no water; on other days, the gas or electricity goes. To live here you live inside a national body, the scent of cologne, urinals and sugar everywhere, sugar being a useful substance for keeping a population somewhat peppy. It seems that only on certain government-decreed days the chickens lay and you find hundreds of people gleeful as they carry gray open trays of eggs home for safekeeping. At scheduled hours, bread appears in the bakeries and every passerby hoists a triumphant loaf of fifty grams, no more and no less. Every restaurant's menu lists tantalizing items that will never be obtained by anyone.

As legend would have it, the people, however, are mostly a constant party.

In this travel, its deprivations and pleasures, I seem still to be performing some kind of wake for my father, a man who always managed, in his way, to find gold in dirt.

This hotel from where I write is a sybarite's enclave in an uneasy socialist utopia. As if I have just crawled out of some gasless, waterless outback, I deeply appreciate its café con leche. The months here have made it easy to recognize travelers from Berkeley, flocked here in disproportionate number: they talk out of the corners of their mouths as if their next restless thought tugs for flight. If they are older, they are fit and wear practical many-pocketed vests and floppy hats, their gestures loose and expressive. If younger, they are tattooed, hefty in calf muscle and committed to years of travel, either as foreign guides in Latin America or still fighting the good fight for Che's idea of the new man motivated by moral profit and not financial gain.

On this early Sunday morning, over the loudspeaker comes, on endlessly hopeful loop, a Muzak version, replete with Andean pipes and a rumba swing, of the one American song ubiquitous in Cuba, the Eagles' "Hotel California":

There she stood in the doorway
I heard the mission bell
I was thinking to myself
This could be heaven or this could be hell

In a purgatory of exile, movement, and endless hope, having carried no more than the government-mandated forty-five pounds of luggage into this country, light-handed and skimming the earth, I recognize: right now I am probably as close as I could possibly be to my father's California, that rosy future and its impossible state, the one I'm pointed toward, the one that can never be.

ACKNOWLEDGMENTS

To Stan for inspired understanding, to Eliana for brilliant insight, to Dalia for joyful depth.

To my first family and to Mae Ziglin Meidav.

Thanks to the meaning offered by friends, teachers and students; the community granted by Kristen, Sarah, Ariel, and Sarabande; Joy; the faith of Brad and Micaela at *Conjunctions* and Laura and Oscar at *Zyzzyva*. Thanks to *The Millions, Guernica/PEN, The Common, The Chicago Tribune*, Terra Nova Books/MIT Press, *The Kenyon Review, Fifth Wednesday Journal, Chattahoochee Review, Bard Papers, Big Big Wednesday, The Massachusetts Review, The American Literary Review*, and other sites for publishing prior versions of many pieces.

Thanks to the University of Massachusetts at Amherst, the Lannan Foundation, the Howard Foundation, the Whiting Foundation, the Bard Fiction Prize, the Kafka Prize from the University of Rochester, Fundación Valparaíso, Cummington Community of the Arts, the Fulbright Commissions of Sri Lanka and Cyprus, VSC, Yaddo, and the MacDowell Colony.

Edie Meidav is the author of three novels—*The Far Field*, *Crawl Space*, and *Lola, California*. Her honors include a Lannan Fellowship, the Kafka Prize for Best Novel by an American Woman, the Bard Fiction Prize, a Whiting Research Award, and a Howard Fellowship. She teaches in the University of Massachusetts-Amherst MFA program.

Sarabande Books is a nonprofit literary press located in Louisville, KY, and Brooklyn, NY. Founded in 1994 to champion poetry, short fiction, and essay, we are committed to creating lasting editions that honor exceptional writing. For more information, please visit sarabandebooks.org.